TREATS

By

CANDI HEART

PINARD HOUSE
PUBLISHING

PRINTED IN THE UNITED STATES OF AMERICA

ISBN-13: 978-1985349391

ISBN-10: 1985349396

Acknowledgements

Cover Art by Kellie Dennis at Book Cover By Design

Co-authored by Cassie Alexandra

Copyediting and Formatting by C.J. Pinard

Other books in the *Sexy Lips and Curvy Hips* Series:

Racing Hearts

Walking Dick

Love Handles

Big Escapes

Sweet Treats

Chapter 1

You're amazing, do you know that?" my fiancé, Sonny, murmured against my neck as he stood behind me. It was his thirty-second birthday and I'd just finished putting the final touches on his favorite breakfast—cinnamon, apple, and pecan crepes.

"Admit it. You're marrying me for my cooking," I replied, smiling up at him over my shoulder.

Sonny's hands slipped to my chest. "Among other things."

I slapped his hands away and turned around. "Don't start something you have no time to finish."

He smiled wickedly. "I could skip breakfast?"

As much as I would have enjoyed a quick romp with him, I knew he had meetings all day and would be extremely irritable if he skipped eating. It certainly wouldn't fair well on a day like today. His company, *Business Attire Outfitters*, was being audited. If that wasn't stressful enough, his soon-to-be-ex-wife, Natalie, was refusing to sign off on their divorce papers, so he also had to meet with the lawyers in the afternoon. They'd been separated for over two years and he claimed she was doing everything in her power to make his life a living hell. I'd never met the woman, but had heard all about her antics. If just being a bitch wasn't bad enough, they also had a daughter together and she even used her as leverage when things weren't going her way.

"We have all night for that." I slid my hands around his neck. "And because it's your birthday, I have a couple special surprises for you later."

His eyebrows shot up. "You do? What?"

I wasn't about to tell him about the red teddy I'd purchased. Or the expensive bottle of champagne. Or the decadent chocolate cake I'd spent three days perfecting.

"You'll just have to wait and see."

He gave me a pouty look. "It's going to be a long day and I could use something to keep my spirits up. Besides, you know how much I hate surprises."

"Yes, and too bad. These particular surprises will be worth the wait. I promise."

He smiled. "Maybe I should tickle them out of you."

My eyes narrowed. "Don't you dare."

I *hated* being tickled, especially by him. He was a little too rough and wouldn't stop until I was almost in tears. He'd been the youngest of three brothers and I had a feeling they'd done the same to him, creating the damnable Tickle Monster.

Sonny raised his hands in the air and scrunched his neck down. "Here comes the... Tickle Monster!"

I quickly grabbed his plate of food and handed it to him. "You'd better eat these before they get cold, Tickle Monster." I looked at the clock. "Plus, it's getting late and I still have to get ready for work. I have a wedding cake to finish before noon."

He checked the time. "Shit, you're right. You should eat something. I really can't eat all of this by myself and it's too tasty to go to waste," he replied, the Tickle Monster temporarily forgotten. "Let's share it."

I looked down at the sinfully delicious platter of crepes and fought the temptation. One simple bite could throw me off track. "I can't. I'm on this new diet. Remember?"

2

He gave me a half smile. "Oh, yeah. The soup one, right?"

The diet he was referring to was two months back and I was already onto something new. One could only eat so much cabbage and broth. Admittedly, I'd lost ten pounds, but had spent more time on the toilet than I cared to admit. After tiring of the soup, I gained the weight back and then some.

"No. This is the gluten-free one."

He gave me a scornful look. "Sounds like another gimmick. How's it going?"

"I just started it yesterday. It's too early to tell. I noticed you've been losing weight," I replied, glancing down at his gray suit. It definitely looked looser, especially around the middle. Like me, Sonny had been told by his doctor to lose weight, although he only had about twenty pounds to shed. I wanted to lose at least thirty, and that was just in my breasts alone. Like my mother, I'd been cursed with a huge rack and all of the back pain that went along with it. She'd had a breast reduction fifteen years ago, and claimed it was the best thing she'd ever done for herself. If it wasn't for Sonny's fascination with my chest, I'd probably do the same thing. But he did the pouty face whenever I broached the subject. He was apparently a 'breast-man' and claimed that he'd be devastated if I made them any smaller. Of course, losing weight would help to shrink them, which was one of the main reasons for me dieting.

He grinned. "I have. Fifteen pounds, actually."

"How?"

"I just haven't been hungry lately," he said, sitting down at the counter with his crepes. "And I joined a gym."

I stared at him in surprise. "When?"

3

"Last week. I told you I was thinking about it. It's the one in my office building that opened up last year."

"When do you have time to even go? You're always working."

He shrugged. "I do it during my lunch hour."

Imagining him all sweaty in one of his expensive suits, I made a face. "Your poor coworkers."

Sonny snorted. "Very funny. They *have* showers."

"What do you wear?"

"What everyone else wears when they work out—a T-shirt and a pair of shorts. Haven't you noticed them in the washing machine?"

"No. Anna's been doing our laundry."

Anna, our neighbor, was also our housekeeper. She lived with her mother, Janet, who'd recommended her. We didn't really need a housekeeper, but Janet had confided in me about Anna's financial struggles. After learning that she cleaned homes for a living, I immediately hired her to clean ours—three days a week—and paid her well for it.

"Ah. That's right. You mentioned she was helping out. How's she doing?"

"Great." Our condo was cleaner than it had ever been. I could run my finger over anything and not find a trace of dust.

"That's good. I've passed her by in the hallways. She seems like a nice gal."

"She is. You know, maybe I should get a membership at your gym, too? We could work out together." My bakery was only a few blocks away, too, and I'd been considering joining a gym for some time.

4

"I don't know if you'd like it, to be honest," he replied. "They don't have a lot of cardio equipment. Mostly weights and stuff." He grinned. "I doubt you'd want to start lifting."

"Why not? I hear that weight training is great for the metabolism."

"Oh yeah?" he said, shoveling a forkful of crepes into his mouth.

"Yes. You continue to burn calories long after you're done, too," I added, remembering it mentioned in an article I'd read somewhere.

"If you want to, I guess. We wouldn't be able to work out together, if that's your main motivation. I usually try and fit what I can in during my lunch period and you're usually at the bakery around that time."

I sighed. "Yeah, I suppose you're right."

"You were talking about joining that online diet support group. What was that called again?"

"*Curvy Hips and Sexy Lips,*" I replied.

"Yeah, that's it. I bet they'll help you find a gym closer to home. One that will offer aerobic classes and other things you'd enjoy. Not just weight training. Maybe you could even find a workout buddy?"

I wanted *him* to be my workout buddy.

"I suppose."

"Babe, these crepes are delicious. Are you sure you don't want any?" he asked before taking another bite.

"They're all yours," I said, walking over to him. I leaned over and kissed him on the head, where his hair also appeared to be getting thinner. I didn't mind, though. Hair or not, Sonny was mine and I loved the man. "I'm going to get ready for work. You have a wonderful day and don't forget about all of the surprises I have in store for you later." I winked. "I think you're going to like them."

He grinned. "I can't wait. You're so good to me. Too good."

I patted his shoulder. "You're worth it."

Boy, would he ever prove me wrong...

Chapter 2
Mason

Staring down at the letter, I grunted and crumpled it up in my fist. More threats from some wacko named *John*. Apparently, he blamed me for his wife leaving him. I'd never even met John, or the woman who broke his heart, but psycho-boy thought otherwise. Apparently, I was the cause of all of his misfortune and he was threatening to end his bad luck, once and for all.

"This is the fifth letter threatening your life," Mack, my manager said. "I think we need to take this seriously."

"Find out who he is. I'll deal with him *seriously*," I replied as the bedroom door opened up, revealing the curvy blonde, Chelsey, I'd brought back to the hotel suite a few hours earlier. I was the lead singer of a band called *My Life In Chaos*, and we were in Florida. We'd just finished the third stop in our world tour and I'd met Chelsey at the after-party. We'd started talking, and I eventually asked if she wanted to get some breakfast somewhere. Unlike a lot of the women I'd met recently, she'd been able to hold an intelligent conversation and I'd wanted to continue it. Unfortunately, the moment we got into my limo, she showed her true colors and was just as bad as all the other star-struck groupies who followed us around. She even offered to give me a blowjob, or whatever else I wanted, because I was her favorite celebrity. Of course, it was late and I took her up on the offer. I might have been disappointed, but I was still a man, and passing up a free B.J. wasn't in my DNA. Especially since I was single. So, instead of breakfast, we'd ended up in my hotel bed, drinking and having sex until sunrise.

Mack ignored Chelsey, who still looked good despite the bed-head and smudged mascara. "The hell you will. You're not getting within fifty feet of that wacko," he said.

"Hey, Chelsey. Sleep okay?" I asked, already itching for her to leave. The sex had been good, but there was nothing else I wanted from her. Especially now that I was sober and thinking more clearly.

"Yes. Very," she replied, smiling brightly. "I can't believe it's already noon. Did you want to grab lunch somewhere?"

"Sorry, I've got to get to the airport soon," I lied. "I'll have my limo driver take you home."

Her smile fell and she sighed in disappointment. "Seriously?"

"Mason, about that letter. Don't worry about it. I'll take care of it," Mack said, standing up. "Just don't go anywhere without checking in with me first."

I gave him a scornful smile. "Do I ever?"

"Don't even go there," he replied, heading toward the door. "You're always sneaking out. That needs to stop. It's for your own protection."

He was probably right, but I was sick of being babysat. Soon he'd have security handing me toilet paper.

"I hear you," I replied, stretching my legs out in front of me.

"I know you *hear* me. I just wish you'd take me seriously," he said, giving me one last look.

"Bye, Mackie-pooh," I said, blowing him a kiss.

Chelsey giggled.

Mack grunted and walked out.

"You sure you have to take off so soon?" Chelsey asked, batting her eyelashes at me.

There was no way I wanted to go another round with her. I already regretted our night together. Unlike a lot of guys in my situation, having chicks throw themselves at me, just because I was famous, was a turnoff.

"Sorry, hon. Like I said, I'm in a hurry and right now, it's business before pleasure, unfortunately. I'll call my driver," I said, picking my cell phone up from the coffee table.

She didn't look very happy. "So," Chelsey huffed. "I guess that's it? I bet it also means you won't be calling me either."

"If I'm ever in Florida, I'll try and look you up."

"Right," she said dryly. She slung her purse over her shoulder and headed toward the doorway. "Don't bother with the limo. I'll find my own way home."

Relieved, I watched her walk out the door and turned on the television. Women like her were a dime-a-dozen and I was tired of shopping at the Goodwill.

I seriously needed to change my shopping habits…

Chapter 3

Terra

Four hours after leaving the condo, I stood in my bakery, *Sweet Treats*, frosting pink and yellow roses onto a four-tiered wedding cake, when my cell phone rang. It was Sonny.

"Hi, babe," he said and sighed. "I hate to say this, but I'm probably going to be home later than planned. It's this damn auditing thing."

I groaned. "How much later? We have dinner reservations, remember?"

I'd been able to get us a table at a ritzy restaurant in Minneapolis called The Marble Horse. He'd been dying to go there for ages, but it was usually impossible to score reservations, as they were always booked out months in advance. Fortunately, the cake I was working on at the moment was for the head maître d's daughter. She'd somehow worked us in, and I hadn't yet told Sonny. It was one of the big surprises.

"I don't know. Probably an hour, tops."

That was doable. I relaxed. "Okay."

"Maybe we should meet at the restaurant?"

I bit the corner of my lip. "No. I'd rather not. I want the restaurant to be a total surprise."

"I know, but if things don't go as quickly as planned, you might not have a choice but to meet me there."

He was right. Reservations were for seven o'clock, and

with my luck, the restaurant would give them away if we didn't arrive sharply.

I tapped my foot, mulling it over. There was no sense in spilling the beans if we didn't know whether or not he was going to be late. We had time. "Why don't you just call me at six and let me know what's happening? Or, maybe I could pick you up in front of your building?"

"I don't want to leave my new Beemer in the parking ramp. Not with all of the recent robberies happening lately in the area."

I sighed. "I understand."

"Listen, babe, I'll call you when I have a better of idea of when I can leave and we'll figure things out then. Okay?"

"Fine."

"I have to go. I have another call coming in. It's probably my lawyer."

"Okay. I love—"

He hung up.

I set my phone down and began doing some stretches. I'd been hunched over the cake for so long, my back was killing me. I bent down to try and crack it, when I heard a sound nobody ever wants to hear—unless it's during a wild round of sex. It was the sound of fabric ripping.

Groaning, I stood up straight and reached under my smock to feel around. Sure enough, I'd split the seam down the back of my new slacks. The ones I'd paid a hundred dollars for because I thought they actually kind of flattered my ass. Now the damn things didn't even cover it.

"You've got to be kidding me," I growled, trying to pull the fabric over my exposed skin. Luckily, I wore a long enough smock which covered it, but I needed to change.

Marcella, my aunt and manager of the bakery, rushed into the back room. "What's wrong?"

I scowled. "I ripped my new pants."

"Dammit to hell. How?" she asked, looking me up and down.

"I leaned over to crack my back," I replied, embarrassed. "And my other crack decided to make an appearance."

Marcella's lips pursed together as she tried not to laugh.

"Go ahead and laugh. I would too if it was the other way around."

"I'm sorry. It's not funny," she said, laughing.

My aunt was a skinny twig and looked a lot like Jane Fonda, only with bright-red hair. She had no idea of what it was like to experience the kind of humiliation heavier women sometimes did. Of course, she had Tourette 's syndrome, so her life wasn't all peaches and cream, either. With her tics, shoulder shrugging, rapid blinking, and occasional bouts of profanity, my weight problem was trivial compared to the everyday bullshit she dealt with. One time, a customer even accused her of being possessed by demons. The crazy woman had actually pulled out a cross and tried doing an exorcism on Marcella because she kept saying, 'dammit to hell', which usually the extent of her cursing. On special occasions, she might add in the F-word, but it was rare. Fortunately, Marcella wasn't the sensitive sort. In fact, instead of getting humiliated, she cussed the woman out of the bakery and then laughed about it with the other customers, who were mostly regulars.

"Shit happens," Marcella said with a shrug.

"Yeah. Story of my life," I muttered. "I'm going to finish

this cake and then run home to change." I looked at the clock. "Cindy should be in soon, too. Can you handle it here by yourself for a while?"

She snorted. "Me? Of course."

"I figured you could, but I had to ask."

"I'd better get back to the register."

I picked up the frosting wand. "I'll let you know when I'm leaving."

Marcella was about to walk out of the kitchen when she turned back around. "It's Sonny's birthday today, isn't it?"

I smiled at her. "Yeah."

"Tell him happy birthday from me, okay?"

"Sure."

"We haven't seen him around much lately," she said.

"He's been really busy."

The front door chimed, indicating a customer had arrived.

"Dammit to hell," she said. "I got it."

An hour later, I was unlocking the door to my condo, when I heard laughter.

I froze. I cocked my ear to the door and heard it again.

Realizing it was Anna's laugh, I blew out a breath and stepped inside. I took off my shoes, and then went to go find her to let her know I was home. As I headed down the hallway, I heard her in the bathroom, saying something.

Thinking she might be on the phone, I raised my hand to knock when I heard another voice inside with her.

"Bend over," he said.

My stomach dropped when I realized it was Sonny's voice.

"That's it, baby. Spread your cheeks for me," he said huskily.

"Like this?" Anna asked.

"Wider. That's it. Oh, baby, you've got a nice little ass."

"What the flying fuck?" I whispered in horror. I couldn't believe the man I loved was saying such things to another woman.

Anna giggled on the other side of the door. "Stop. You're too rough."

"Bend over. I'll show you rough," he growled.

Nauseated, I felt like my heart had been ripped out of my chest and then shoved into a meat grinder.

How could he?

As I pictured them together, my heartbreak turned into insurmountable rage. I threw open the door to confront them and immediately regretted it. From that very moment, I knew I'd never, ever forget the image of Anna, bent over my bathroom sink with Sonny behind her, his pants down around his ankles.

Seeing me, the two of them gasped.

"Terra. What are you doing home?" Sonny asked, quickly pulling his trousers.

"I live here, you asshole!" I screamed, tears streaming down my face. "Dammit to hell…!"

Chapter 4

Terra

Six Months Later

T erra, you have a call on line three," Marcella called into the kitchen.

I set down my spatula and grabbed the phone. "This is Terra."

"Girl, I have been trying to text you all day long. Are you ghosting me, or what?"

I smiled. My best friend, Celine, hated to be kept waiting, for even a minute. Especially when she was excited about something. From the tone of her voice, she had some big news for me. "Sorry, I've been so busy trying to get this birthday cake done, I haven't checked my phone. What's going on?"

"I scored four tickets to the *My Life In Chaos* concert this weekend!" she cried out. "Can you believe it, Terrabae? We get to see Mason Stone perform live onstage!"

"How in the world did you manage to do that?" I asked, incredulous.

Mason Stone was already a rock legend, and he'd only been around for four or five years. With several platinum records under his belt, plus a couple movie appearances, the man was a mega superstar. Last year, the magazines even labeled him as "The Most Sexiest Man In Hollywood."

"Jimmy got them for me since my birthday is Sunday."

Her husband, Jimmy, worked in the music industry. He helped set up tours and events in the Twin Cities.

"That's great. I'm sure you'll have a lot of fun."

"No, girl… I don't think you were listening. *We* are going to have a lot of fun. I'm inviting you and my sisters."

I felt a rush of excitement at the idea, which quickly turned to dread. I hadn't been to a concert in ages and I didn't really feel like going out in public. I'd gained fifteen pounds since kicking Sonny out of our condo. I'd neglected my hair, my skin, even my nails—which I'd recently developed a habit of chewing. I was a young woman already heading down the path of old maid-slash-cat lady—minus the cats.

"Terra. Did you hear me? I'm sending a limo to your place on Saturday, around six. We are going to this thing in style, so be prepared."

"Oh crap… I can't make it," I lied. "I'm sorry."

She snorted. "Don't even go there with me. I already talked to you about getting together this Saturday. Remember? You said you were going to clear your schedule and we were going to celebrate my birthday. So this concert is what we're going to do."

I groaned inwardly. "I know, but—"

"I *know* what this is about. You're still depressed about Sonny. Don't get me wrong; what he did was awful. It was despicable. But, you *have* to move on."

"I am. I mean, I'm trying. Really."

"We've been friends since the fifth grade, and I call bullshit. You might be trying something, but it's not anything healthy."

She was right. The only thing I'd been trying were the forty decadent flavors of Ben & Jerry's. But I couldn't help it. I was still so heartbroken about Sonny's affair. Even worse, I'd learned that they were still together. I'd caught him leaving her condo the other day, and as if that wasn't bad enough, we'd had to ride down the elevator together. *Talk about awkward.* He'd tried apologizing again for hurting me while I stood there trying to maintain some dignity by acting like I didn't care. The moment they'd stepped out of the elevator, however, I'd bawled my eyes out.

"Terrabae?"

I sighed. She was right. I had promised to do something with her for her birthday. I couldn't allow myself to spoil her fun because I was still feeling sorry for myself. "I'm here."

"I'm not going to let you sit home and wallow in another weekend of self-pity parties. You are going with us and I won't take 'no' for an answer. You got it?"

"Yes."

"It's for your own good."

I sighed.

"Now, remember… six o'clock we'll be by to pick you up and you're *going* to have a good time. That's an order."

"Okay."

"Good. No backing out, either. You do and I'll drag your ass out of your place myself. You know I can do it, too."

Celine definitely could. She was a large woman, even bigger than myself, and as strong as an ox. I once saw her pick up her husband Jimmy, who had to weigh about two bills, and toss him in their swimming pool like it was nothing.

17

"I won't back out," I promised.

"You'd better not. So, what you going to wear?"

Good question.

"I don't know. I might have to get something new." Although I hated the thought of going up another size, I really didn't have anything nice to wear because of the extra weight I'd put on. Sweats and a hoodie definitely weren't going to cut it, either. Knowing Celine and her sisters, they'd all be decked out in something sexy and expensive.

"Do it. Treat yourself. You know I did. By the way, I wanted to wait to surprise you, but since I can tell that you're still on the fence about going, I figured I should tell you now… we have backstage passes to meet Mr. Hotness himself."

My eyes widened. "Mason Stone?"

She squealed like a teenager. "Yes!"

I had to admit, that *was* kind of exciting.

"Sounds like fun."

"*Fun*? We are going to have the time of our lives. Prepare to party your ass off. This might be a birthday present for me, but it's also my gift to you."

I didn't see it as a gift, but appreciated the sentiment. I would have much rather sat home and watched reruns of *Grey's Anatomy* or *This Is Us.*

"Oh, I gotta go. I'm at Cossetta's and I think Jimmy might be trying to text me. We're having lunch together."

"Yum," I said, my stomach growling. Cossetta's was an Italian restaurant in St. Paul and had the best pizza and pasta. "Have fun."

We talked for a few more seconds and then hung up. I walked over to the sink to wash my hands just as Marcella stepped into the kitchen.

"Maria is here and we're going to lunch. She's up front if you want to chat before we leave."

I cringed inwardly. I loved my mother, but the last time we spoke, it had ended up in an argument. She'd dropped by my condo unexpectedly and had started nagging. First, it had been about my place, which admittedly, had been a mess. Then about my added weight, which apparently worried her more than me. Finally, about me being depressed. She wanted me to talk to a therapist, and when I refused, she suggested I at least open up to her.

"I'm your mother. You can talk to me about anything. Please, let me try and help," she'd begged.

So I opened up, and afterward, she gave me the same advice as everyone else: "Move on. He's not worth being miserable over."

Then she started in with, "You're stronger than you know. You're like me. I'm a survivor and so are you."

If only I was more like her...

My mother and I were like night and day. She was thin, beautiful, and seemed to skate though life. She'd never had her heart broken. Not by someone who could have prevented it, at least. Happily married for twenty years to my father, they'd seemed to have the perfect life. At least until he died of a brain aneurism. As far as I knew, that had been the one major hiccup in her life, but she *was* a strong woman and had picked herself back up fairly quickly. Eventually, she met up with an old friend from high school, a woman named Jackie. I wasn't even sure how it happened, but a year later, Mom decided she was gay and the two of them moved in together.

Who knew?

Now they were partners and in a solid relationship. I couldn't imagine either of them cheating on each other, so she had no concept of what I was feeling. I actually felt like Sonny had died and I was in mourning, grieving for a man I'd loved. Even worse, for a love that had obviously only been one-sided.

"Yeah," I said, removing my smock. "I'd better or she'll come back here and give me the third degree."

Marcella sighed. "She's only worried about you."

"I know."

I followed Marcella to the front of the bakery, where my mother was talking to one of the cashiers, Cindy. When she spotted me, Mom smiled and asked if I wanted to join them for lunch.

"I wish I could, but I'm trying to finish a birthday cake," I said and nodded toward the clock above the donut case. "They're picking it up in an hour."

"That's too bad. Hopefully next time then. By the way, Jackie and I were wondering if you wanted to come over for dinner on Sunday. Her nephew is going to be in town and we invited him. Along with the neighbors."

"Tyler?" I asked, groaning inwardly.

They'd been trying to set me up with him for years. Even before Sonny showed up in my life. We'd never met, but I'd seen a picture of him. He was thirty-six, a dentist, with nice, white teeth, and warm blue eyes. He was also tall and rail-thin, to the point of looking emaciated. I needed a man with some meat on his bones. Tyler looked as if a gust of wind could blow him all the way to China.

"Yes. He wants to meet you. I hope you'll come," she said, pleading with her eyes.

"Mom! I'm not interested in Tyler. I told you that before."

"You don't have to go out with him. We just want you two to meet. You're practically family."

Right. If my mother had her way, Tyler and I would be married this time next year.

"To be honest, I'm going to a concert Saturday night. I'm not driving and I'm sure I'll be out late. I'll probably want to rest Sunday."

Her eyes widened and she smiled. "You're going to a concert?"

I told her about the call from Celine.

"*My Life In Chaos*? I actually like a couple of their songs," my mother replied. "And you have backstage passes to meet them?"

"Apparently," I said.

"I am *so* jealous," Cindy said. "The lead singer is *so* hot." She fanned herself with the check she was about to shove into the register. "Ya know, I tried getting tickets, but they sold out right away."

"That's too bad," I replied.

She shrugged. "Eh. They'll be back."

"I hope you have a lot of fun, Terra," Marcella said, grabbing her purse from under the counter.

"Thanks. It's not really my thing, but it's Celine's birthday. I promised I'd go."

"You should," my mother said. "And just remember, if you change your mind about Sunday, we'd love to have you over. I'm even making your favorite dish—lasagna." Her eyes twinkled, and in a sing-song voice, she enticed me with, "It's Grandpa Angelo's recipe."

My stomach growled just thinking about it. My grandfather, Angelo Bertolliano, used to own his own Italian restaurant. Growing up, my parents and I would eat there every Friday night and I'd almost always order the lasagna. There was nothing else like it in the world.

"I'll think about it," I said. "But, I'm serious, Mother. I do not want you to even *think* about trying to set Tyler and me up."

"Cross my heart," she said, making the sign across her chest. "I won't. We just want our families to get to know each other. Besides, he lives in Florida. It would never work out between you anyway."

I relaxed. "Okay."

"Come on, Maria," Marcella said, walking toward the front door. "I need to eat, dammit to hell. All this talk about lasagna is making me hungry."

"Have fun Saturday," my mother said, following her. She looked back over her shoulder at me. "Call me Sunday. No matter what. I want to hear all about your evening."

"I will," I replied.

As the two of them walked out, a tall, broad-shouldered guy wearing a gray hoodie held the door for them. They both thanked him and then he stepped into the bakery.

"Wow," he said, walking up to the large dessert case in front of Cindy. "These all look incredible. I think I've just died and gone to heaven."

"We offer samples, too," Cindy replied, and then did a double take at him. Her eyes grew wide. "Oh, my God! You

22

look exactly like Mason Stone. We were just talking about him, too." She jutted her thumb behind her at me.

He chuckled and pushed the hood away from his dark-brown hair, and then waved a dismissive hand. "Eh, people tell me that all the time. I'd love to have his money though! Right? I'd have bodyguards and a fancy car parked outside."

"Oh yeah. Of course," she replied, laughing nervously.

I stepped closer to Cindy for a better view, and had to admit, he definitely looked like Mason Stone. Only this guy was even cuter, if it were possible. He had a broad chest, a light smattering of dark stubble on his face, and startling blue eyes. Noticing me, he gave a lopsided grin that transformed his sharp, chiseled face into something that could only be described as raw, masculine beauty.

"Do you have any donuts left?" he asked me and then looked back down at the case filled with pastries and cupcakes. "Not that I wouldn't love to try one of these cupcakes or even a tart. I've just been craving chocolate Bavarian crème donuts. Tell me you have those." He looked back up at me.

"You're in luck, we do. They're over here," I said, stepping around the glass case. I walked over to the donuts and pointed toward the left side of the case, at two rows of chocolate-covered Long Johns and Bismarcks. "These all have Bavarian crème filling."

"What about those?" he asked, nodding toward the other side of the case, which also contained Long Johns.

"They don't have filling."

"None at all?"

I shook my head.

"I don't understand why anyone would want a Long John

without crème. That's just too much donut and no prize in the middle."

I grinned up at him. "Some people just don't like filling. I'm with you, though. I have to have the cream."

His lip twitched. "So how much would it cost for a dozen donuts?"

"It depends on which ones you want," Cindy said, now standing next to us.

"Oh. I see," he replied, looking up at the hand-written pricing board high above the register.

"I can help him. I know you're trying to get that cake done in back," Cindy said and then when he turned around, she pretended to fan herself.

Cindy was right. The man *was* gorgeous. Too attractive for someone like me, but not for a gal like her. She'd just turned twenty-one, was skinny and blonde, with perfect skin and hair. Plus, she almost always smelled like apples. As for me, my scent-of-the-day usually consisted of fryer grease or bleach. There was nothing flattering about it.

"Okay. Thanks, Cindy," I replied and turned to walk back around the counter.

"Hey, thank you for your help," the stranger called out.

I looked back and smiled. "No problem. Thank you for stopping in today."

"Are you the owner?"

"I am."

A couple walked into the store and asked if we sold coffee.

"Yes," Cindy said and then stepped away to help them.

24

"Seriously, I think I may have found my new favorite bakery," he said, his eyes lowering, "Wow. Those have to be the biggest muffins I've ever seen."

His bold statement left me speechless, but then I remembered there were jumbo blueberry and banana muffins in the case behind me.

"Yeah. They're rather big," I said, smiling weakly.

"So," he grinned, "you make cakes, too, huh," he glanced at the name stitched on my apron, "Terra?"

I noticed the gleam in his eyes and had to wonder if he knew I'd thought he'd been talking about my breasts. "Yes."

He craned his head around. "Do you have a cake book anywhere? I might have to order one."

"Yes, I have a couple of them," I replied, walking toward the counter where I kept the albums. "What's the occasion?"

"My birthday is coming up."

"Nice. Well, if you don't find what you're looking for in the albums, I also do special requests," I said.

He grinned. "I'm getting picky in my old age, so I might take you up on that."

I chuckled. "Old age? How old are you? Twenty-five?"

"I'll be thirty," he replied. "What about you?"

"Twenty-six."

Smiling, he rubbed his chin. "I thought so."

"You *thought* I was twenty-six? Exactly? Not twenty-seven or twenty-five?"

"Nope. Twenty-six. You have that, 'I'm over a quarter of a century old' look. But, only slightly. And I mean, very slightly."

25

I laughed. "Okay. That has to be the weirdest thing anyone has said to me. Today."

"Wait until you get to know me better. You'll forget what normal people are like," he said softly.

As much as I would have enjoyed getting to know him better, I knew he was just making conversation. "Normal people are overrated, right?"

"I don't know. You seem pretty normal, but in a good way."

"Thank you. I think?"

He was definitely an odd duck. But a very attractive one who'd made me laugh more times in the last couple minutes than I had in the last few months.

The phone rang as the coffee couple walked out of the bakery.

"Terra, why don't you get that and I'll help him?" Cindy said, walking back over to us. "I know how busy you are right now."

"Okay. It was nice meeting you," I said, before heading to the phone.

He winked. "You, too."

Chapter 5

Mason

I hated lying to them, but I'd snuck out of my hotel for a jog, and the last thing I needed was for it to get out that I was wandering the streets of Minneapolis. Especially without security. If Mack learned about it, I'd never hear the end of it.

"So, do you live around here?" the cute blonde asked, when Terra disappeared into the back room.

"Kind of."

I'd actually grown up in Minneapolis, so it wasn't a complete lie. Unfortunately, I had no idea where my old man was living now.

My mother died when I was a fourteen, and had Dad turned to the bottle and never looked back. He and booze were a toxic combination. Not only did he have blackouts, he'd often become violent. Fortunately, he'd stopped drinking when I was a baby, mostly because my mother had been a strong-willed, no-nonsense Irish woman who'd refused to put up with his shit. But her death had hit him hard and he didn't just fall off the wagon, he dove off head-first.

First, it was mainly the evenings, when he'd get home from work and drink a six-pack. It quickly progressed to getting shit-faced every weekend at the local bar. Eventually, he couldn't hold a job because he was constantly drunk. The only reason we'd been able to keep the house as long as we had was because of Mom's life insurance policy. Those days had been miserable for the both of us, especially me. Not only did I lose my mother, but also my old man.

I answered her vaguely, my mind still on Dad. The last I'd heard, our family home had been foreclosed upon, and that was four years ago. Although there was a lot of bad history between the two of us, if I knew where to find him, I'd try and help him out. But he had pretty much disappeared without a trace. I currently didn't know if he was dead or living under a bridge.

"So, your birthday is coming up. Are you planning your own party, or what?" she asked as I paged through one of the cake books.

"God, no. I hate parties. I love cake, though," I glanced at her nametag, "Cindy." I replied, smiling at the girl, but I couldn't stop thinking about Terra. She'd been stunning, especially those big, green eyes of hers.

"Yeah. Everyone needs cake for their birthday." She coiled a strand of blonde hair around her finger and gave me a flirty smile. "And Terra does make the best ones in town."

"I bet. So, does she own this place with her husband?" I asked, fishing without shame.

"She's not married," Cindy replied. "She *was* engaged, but the asshole cheated on her."

I wondered how Terra would feel if she knew her cashier was giving out information about her, especially, something so private, to a stranger.

"She's better off without him," I said.

"Yeah. That's what I told her, too."

A picture on the wall caught my eye. It was of Terra standing next to a large cake and holding up a plaque. She had on an elegant black dress that hugged her sexy curves. This time, her hair was down in long waves, falling just

28

below her breasts. I suddenly had an image of her naked and staring down at me with that same smile. Picturing my hands on her breasts and her hips moving over mine gave me instant wood.

Fuck.

That's what I got for being abstinent the last couple of months. Sure, I'd had plenty of chances, but was now trying something different with my life. Like, not giving in to every groupie who batted her eyelashes at me during a concert. Being on the road made it hard to meet decent women, but I'd decided to try and keep my zipper up until after the tour. Now, here I was all hot-and-bothered in the middle of the day, at a damn bakery.

Really nice, idiot.

Knowing I needed to calm the tent in my sweatpants, I tore my eyes away from Terra to the cake, which I had to admit was pretty fucking amazing. It was shaped like a medieval castle and even had a moat surrounding it. I couldn't believe how detailed it was and figured that it must have taken her hours to create such an intricate creation. There was even a blue fire-breathing dragon wrapped around one of the towers. Pretty bad-assed looking, too.

"That is absolutely incredible," I said in awe. "I've never seen anything like it. She must have gotten an award, I take it?"

"Yeah. She won second place on a TV show," Cindy said. "Cake Queens."

"I've heard of it," I replied and chuckled. Not having a lot of time for television, I had assumed it had something to do with drag queens. Apparently, I was wrong. "Terra is very talented. She should have won first place."

"Exactly."

My cell phone chimed. I looked and there was a text from Mack, asking me where in the hell I'd disappeared to. Sighing, I ignored it and put my phone away.

"I've got to go. Tell Terra I'll try and make it back in sometime soon. I'd like to talk to her about designing my birthday cake."

Cindy looked disappointed. "Sure. Did you want one of the Long Johns?"

"Next time," I said, walking out the door.

Chapter 6

Terra

After taking the phone call, I found it hard not to go back out to the front. The stranger had been so nice, and of course there was the fact that he was gorgeous. But I knew I had to get the cake done and wasting my time drooling over a guy like him wasn't productive, so I focused on the cake. About ten minutes into my decorating, Cindy walked back into the kitchen.

"Oh, my God, wasn't he hot?" she said, fanning herself. "He *must* be a model or something. If he's not, then he sure as hell should be."

"He was definitely cute."

"I swear, he has to be Mason Stone's doppelganger."

"Did you ever get his name?"

She sighed. "No and he didn't order a cake either. He received some text and then rushed out of here so fast, you'd have thought there was a fire."

I finished the last of the balloons and inspected the cake. It wasn't anything fancy, but exactly what the customer had ordered. "Who knows, maybe he's a firefighter?"

"I could definitely picture him posing for one of those hot firefighter calendars."

I chuckled. "Yeah, I know what you mean. For someone who loves donuts, he looked like he might be pretty ripped under that hoodie."

"Yeah." She twirled a blonde curl around her finger

absently. "I hope he really does comes back. He said he'd like to talk to you personally about ordering a cake. He was pretty fascinated by the castle one you made on *Cake Queens.*"

"He saw the picture, huh?" I asked, remembering that weekend. My aunt had entered me in a cake-decorating contest. She took pictures of some of my designs and sent them without my knowledge. A couple weeks later, the producers of *Cake Queens* called and asked if I was interested in being on television. I'd been reluctant to do it, but thought it would help with business. In the end, it had been a lot of fun, even though I came in second. The first-place contestant deserved the win, however. Her castle had been constructed to look like *Hogwarts*, Harry Potter's school, and she'd done an outstanding job.

Cindy bit the side of her lower lip. "I can't believe he's going to be thirty. He's older than most guys I've dated, but... totally worth it. I mean, if he does stop back in and asks me out, I definitely wouldn't say no."

"He just might," I replied. "You'd make a cute couple."

"We would, wouldn't we?" she replied with a dreamy look in her eyes.

The bell jingled in the front of the bakery.

Her eyes widened. "Yikes, maybe he's back..." she said and disappeared out of the kitchen.

Smiling to myself, I put some finishing touches on the cake and then packaged it up. Afterward, as I washed my hands in the sink, I stared at my reflection in the mirror and frowned. I really did need to do something about my hair. It was a wreck. Personally, I thought my long hair had always been my best feature, but I'd been neglecting it since my split with Sonny.

I sighed.

My mother and friends were right—I needed to move on. Wallowing in self-pity wasn't ever going to bring him back to me. Nor did I even want that. At least I was still attracted to other men. The one from earlier had proven that. I'd even gotten a few butterflies. Of course, a gorgeous guy like that would do it to anyone.

I decided to make a hair appointment and called around. Fortunately, I was able to find someone who could fit me in later in the day. As I hung up the phone, I decided to swing by the mall on the way and pick out something to wear for the concert, too. It was time to start thinking about myself and not the things I'd lost.

Two hours later, I walked into Macy's and began looking for an outfit I'd feel comfortable in, but would still look somewhat classy. Being so damn top-heavy, and having added a few more pounds to my waistline the last few months, made it almost impossible. I tried on several outfits and was practically in tears before I found a semi-slimming black dress that stopped just above my knee. I paired it with a cute, black sequined jacket, a chunky gold and onyx necklace, matching earrings, and new leather pumps. In the end, I spent almost two hundred dollars, which was more than I'd ever allowed myself for an outfit. But it was a special night and I knew Celine would be thrilled to see me all dressed up.

A short time later, I was at the salon and found myself sitting in front of a hairstylist named Sebastian. After telling him what I wanted, he made some recommendations, and then we spent the next two hours chatting while he went to work on my hair.

"So, you've got tickets to see My Life In Chaos, huh?" he said, foiling my hair.

"Yes. We have backstage passes, too, I guess."

"Wow. That's exciting. You know, I actually went to high school with Mason Stone," Sebastian said, a small smile on his face.

"You did? I read somewhere that he grew up in Minneapolis."

"Yes. He was actually pretty quiet in those days. He didn't seem to have a lot of friends either," Sebastian replied. "I think he preferred it that way, in all honesty."

"Really? Why do you say that?"

"Just the way he carried himself. There were rumors that he had it tough at home, so that probably had a lot to do with it. I think his mom died when he was pretty young. I don't know anything about his father, but I'm sure it had to be hard for the both of them."

"I'm sure."

"He was in all of the school plays, though. He was a great actor and we all know the man can sing."

"Yeah."

"What about you? Where'd you go to school?"

"I went to Lakeview."

"Oh, yeah. I had some friends who went to that school. Lots of drama there, I heard."

"You heard right."

I'd graduated a few years behind Sebastian, but he was

right about the drama, among other things. I'd hated it there, mainly because of the way I'd been bullied and harassed. The girls had taunted me about my weight from early on, even back when I only had a few pounds to lose. Then there'd been the other end of the spectrum. Apparently, having big boobs meant you were easy. At least the football team must have thought so because there'd been a time when four players asked me out within days of each other. I'd been thrilled at first, until I was forced to block passes and field-goal attempts during the dates. I later learned from Celine, whose boyfriend had also been on the team, that the guys had been taking bets on who could score with me first. I'd been mortified to the point of wanting to switch schools. But my mother talked me out of it and in the end, I was glad I'd stayed. It taught me to face my fears instead of letting them direct my life.

"If you get a chance to talk to Mason, tell him that Sebastian Hallaway says hi."

"Okay."

I wasn't exactly sure how the backstage passes worked. We'd probably get a quick word with them, or a photo-op. But I liked Sebastian and would try to remember if the opportunity presented itself.

When he was finished with my hair, I was very pleased. Not only did he layer it, but he lightened up the ends, giving my hair an ombre look.

"I love it," I replied, handing him back the mirror after checking out the back of my head.

"Good. You're going to look gorgeous for the concert." He looked at my face and tapped his chin thoughtfully. "Could I make a suggestion, though?"

"Of course."

"Let me shape your eyebrows. Just a little. It'll be on the house."

I glanced at myself in the mirror. I thought they looked fine, but I'd loved what he'd done to my hair and trusted his judgement. "Thank you and of course. Go for it."

He smiled. "I love that you're so agreeable with my suggestions."

"I love what you did to my hair. Something tells me I'm going to be pleased with my eyebrows, too."

After waxing, plucking, and using an eyebrow pencil, Sebastian had me staring in wonder at my reflection. I couldn't believe the difference.

"Your green eyes really dazzle now," he said, smiling in approval. "Damn, I'm good."

I laughed. "Yes. You are. I've definitely found my new, favorite stylist," I replied and then thought of the cute guy from the bakery. He'd said the same thing about my shop. Like me, I hoped he'd meant it.

"Wonderful. Here's my card," he said, snatching one off his station. "Just don't forget to mention my name to Mason. Especially after he falls in love with you. I mean, I did help to bring out your inner goddess. Now you're gorgeous on the outside as well as the inside."

I smiled warmly. "You're so sweet."

He winked. "That's why karma brought us together, gorgeous."

He definitely was a keeper and pretty gorgeous himself. Too bad that the only decent guys I'd been meeting lately were either gay or out of my league.

Chapter 7
Mason

After sneaking back into the hotel, I called Mack and told him I'd been in the pool swimming.

"Next time keep your phone nearby. I almost had management open up your door when you weren't answering," he replied gruffly.

I rolled my eyes. "Well, what's so important that you needed to speak to me?"

"I wanted to remind you about the pre-concert party on Saturday. Make sure you and the guys are ready and not running late."

Isn't that your job?

"I'll be on time, but you're going to have to talk to the others. I'm not their babysitter." I loved my bandmates, but they were immature and needed constant guidance, even while on tour. It was getting so bad that I'd even begun distancing myself from them lately. Especially *after* the concerts, when the real parties occurred. None of them were heavily into drugs, at least I hoped not, but the guys were hard partiers and usually needed a couple of days to sober up afterward.

"They listen to you more than they do to me," Mack said.

"Buy a blow-horn."

He grunted. "Somehow I don't think that will even catch their attention. By the way, I just got word that someone was sneaking around your property last night.

Now that pissed me off. "Who?"

"Not sure. One of the cameras picked him up, but there's no way to identify the trespasser with what he was wearing, I guess."

"Why didn't I get a call about it?"

"Because the security company has my phone number, remember? I don't want you worrying about these things, especially when you're on tour. It's a distraction that would only upset you."

"I'm still upset," I replied angrily. "Waiting to tell me didn't really alleviate any of that."

"Hey, I just found out about it myself. Anyway, the guy took off once the alarm went off. It was probably just some two-bit burglar trying to break in."

"Or maybe it was Stalker John," I replied.

"I didn't want to bring that up, but it's very possible. Just keep an eye out and whatever you do... do *not* leave the hotel by yourself. I mean it, Mason."

"If he's stalking my property in Beverly Hills, I think I'm safe in Minneapolis at the moment."

"The robbery attempt might not be related."

"I'm not going to let an idiot like Stalker John dictate my life."

"He will be doing much more than that if he kills you. He can't do that if you let your security team do their job."

As usual he was being overly dramatic. To appease him, I agreed. Quite frankly, I wanted to confront John on my own and pound some sense into him.

"What are you doing for dinner?" he asked.

"I don't know. Probably just sticking around here."

"You want company?"

"Mack, I think we should keep our relationship platonic," I teased.

He grunted. "I mean, do you want me to invite any chicks? Apparently, some women from one of your fan clubs are staying at the hotel; from what I hear, some of them have some pretty bangin' bodies."

I thought of Terra. Now *she* had a bangin' body.

"No. I'm good."

"Your choice. Let me know if you'd like me to send someone out for food, if you want something different than what's on the hotel menu."

"Thanks. I'll let you know."

We talked for a while longer and then he hung up.

I took a quick shower and climbed down the balcony to the room just below mine, which I'd rented without Mack's knowledge. Lately, he'd been posting a security guard on our floor to keep an eye on things, and I didn't want company. Ten minutes later, I was heading back to the bakery, craving more than just a donut. Unfortunately, Terra had left for the day. Disappointed, I decided it was worth making another trip.

"Tell her I'll be back on Monday. What time does she work?" I asked Cindy, who was batting her eyelashes at me once again.

"She usually gets here around six a.m. and leaves around two," she told me.

"Nice hours," I replied, wondering if I could talk her into grabbing a bite to eat afterward.

"If you like getting up that freaken early," Cindy said. "I'm usually just getting to bed around that time. Especially on the weekends."

"Enjoy it now. When you're my age, you're going to relish your sleep."

"You're not that old," she replied, looking at me like I was crazy.

I just smiled. I may not have looked it, but lately, I was exhausted. The tour, the interviews, the rehearsals, they were really starting to get to me. Not to mention the parties, before and after the concerts. I thoroughly used to enjoy my life. Now I couldn't wait for the end of the tour, just so I could take a breath.

"So, besides ordering a cake, is there something else you want in the bakery?" she asked in a breathless voice.

"Actually, I'll take four of those Long Johns. They're filled, right?"

"Yes," she said, looking disappointed.

I paid for the donuts and asked for Terra's business card. Fortunately, she had her cell phone number listed on it.

"Have a good night," I told Cindy, shoving it into my pocket.

"Thanks, although I'm sure it going to be really boring. I don't have anything to do," she remarked with a helpless smile.

"Lately, those are my favorite kind of nights," I said, as I walked out the door.

Chapter 8

Terra

When I finally made it home, I was exhausted and hungry. I grabbed a chicken pot-pie out of the freezer, and for shits and giggles, looked at the calorie content.

"Tomorrow. I'll start my diet tomorrow," I muttered, staring at the back of the box. Seven-hundred calories for something that wasn't going to fill me up. Not to mention that the carb content was through the roof.

Sighing, I popped it into the microwave and went into the bathroom to check on my hair once again. Fortunately, the wind hadn't blown it all to hell and the pinkness had faded around my eyebrows.

As I was fluffing up my hair, and considering a 'selfie' to post on Facebook—one Sonny might see and realize what he was missing—my phone rang. It was Cindy.

"Guess who stopped in to buy donuts when you were gone?" she said.

"Who?"

"That guy from earlier. The hot one."

"Oh. Did he order a cake?"

"Not yet. He wanted to talk to you about it."

I smiled. "Did you ever get his name?"

"No. I was too flustered. Anyway, he was so nice and we talked for a while about the shop. Call me crazy, but I think he likes me," she said, a smile in her voice.

"Really?" I replied, feeling a little disappointed, not that I didn't want her to be happy. "Did you give him your number?"

"God, no. I couldn't get the nerve up to do something like that. He's going to stop back in early next week and order a cake, though. Maybe he'll ask me for it then?"

She sounded so giddy and excited about the man, I hoped for her sake that he would.

"Oh, I've got to go. Marcella is giving me the evil eye. I just wanted you to know that he stopped back in."

I looked at the clock. It was after seven and the shop closed at eight. "Thanks for letting me know."

"See you tomorrow."

"Okay."

We hung up and I took my pot-pie out of the microwave. I grabbed a Diet Coke out of the refrigerator and turned on the television. As I was flipping through the channels, I noticed that one of the local news stations was talking about *My Life In Chaos* and the upcoming concert. When they flashed a recent picture of the band across the screen, I almost choked on the forkful of food I'd stuffed into my mouth. The man from the bakery looked so much like Mason Stone, it was hard to believe that they weren't the same person. But... they couldn't have been.

Right?

I put the plate of food down, grabbed my phone, and began searching for videos of Mason. Most of the ones were of his music videos and clips from movies.

Sighing, I set my phone down. There was no way Mason Stone had been in my bakery, especially without bodyguards, or a barrage of fans following him. It was crazy to even consider. Plus, he'd been in twice. What kind of a mega superstar would have time to go searching for donuts or ordering a birthday cake?

And... for himself?

His people would have *their* people do all of that stuff for him. Concert or not, the guy wouldn't be roaming the streets of Minneapolis all by his lonesome. No way.

After finishing my dinner, I was still really hungry, but instead of going back into the refrigerator, I turned on my laptop and logged into the *Curvy Hips And Sexy Lips* website. I'd already created an account months before, but hadn't been back since my split with Sonny. I knew I needed motivation to lose weight, so I immediately clicked on some of the weight loss stories. As I scrolled through the articles, I found that some of dieters had lost a significant amount of weight and their "after" pictures were incredible. Unfortunately, it had taken some of them over a year to lose the weight, and that was when I usually lost interest. That being said, I was tired of being envious of everyone else and needed to do something. I decided to try the plan that had been created for me, something called a Keto Diet, and go shopping after work the following day. I'd also try using the expensive cellulite massager thingy I'd purchased after seeing an advertisement for it on Facebook. It looked more like a sex toy, to be honest. I guess you rubbed it across your body, and it was supposed to break up something called fascia, which caused the look of cellulite.

After printing out the grocery list for my new diet, I unboxed the massager and read the directions. Five minutes later, I stood in my shower, briskly rubbing the thing across my stomach, hips, and thighs. After about five minutes, I started getting dizzy and overheated.

"Now I know why you lose weight with this thing," I

mumbled, my arms exhausted from the rapid movements.

I turned off the shower and dried off. As I put my robe on, I noticed that my stomach and thighs were beginning to bruise. I was also feeling slightly nauseous. I literally looked and felt like I'd just gotten the shit kicked out of me.

I grabbed the fat massager and tossed it in the garbage. If this was how some people wanted to lose weight, more power to them. The thing would probably be more efficient *as* a sex toy.

I raised my eyebrow.

Picking it back up, I decided to keep it. There was no sense throwing good money away…

The next couple days seemed long and torturous, especially while I was at work. My low carb intake made me grumpy and I felt like I was starving all day. I couldn't even drink the frozen caramel lattes that I loved so much. Plus, having all of the sugary treats around me didn't help. One time I even absently licked a spatula with frosting on it. Realizing what I'd done, I threw a mini fit, which Marcella heard from the front of the bakery.

"Dammit to hell, what's going on back here?" she asked, rushing into the back.

"I had some frosting," I said, throwing the spatula into the sink. "It threw me out of ketosis, I'm sure."

She frowned. "What the hell is ketosis?"

"To make a long story short, it's a metabolic process that burns stored fat."

"Does this process also make you crabby?"

I narrowed my eyes at her, annoyed. It was one thing to feel grumpy, but it didn't help when someone else pointed it out.

"I'll warn the others," she said, and hurried out of the kitchen.

When Saturday finally arrived, I was in high spirits. I felt better and had even lost a few pounds. Most of it was water weight, I assumed, but my waist felt slimmer and I had more energy. Plus, I was actually looking forward to going out that evening to the concert.

Celine called me earlier in the day, making sure I wasn't planning on canceling on her. After reassuring her that I wouldn't, I rearranged my schedule so that I could leave early. I stopped at Chipotle and ordered a salad, which I'd never done before. As the woman put it together, I stared longingly at the rice, beans, and corn, which wasn't allowed on my diet.

"Anything else?" she asked, looking at me.

I had to bite my tongue to keep from ordering a bag or two of chips. "Just some guacamole."

Mentally patting myself on the back as I walked out of the restaurant, I raced home, scarfed down the Chipotle, and then jumped into the shower. As I lathered up, I noticed there were still some bruises from the fat massager but my body did look a little slender, which I attributed to the Keto diet.

Afterward, I spent the next hour trying to recreate the look that Sebastian had the other day and was quickly reminded of my lack of hair skills. It was why I'd chosen baking school instead of beauty, which had once sounded interesting. Fortunately, my makeup turned out pretty well. I even managed to make the wings on my eyeliner look decent, which was usually a struggle. Especially, if I had coffee beforehand. Once I added the dress, heels, and jewelry, I glanced at my full reflection in the mirror and felt pretty good about myself.

The feeling was short-lived, however.

As I left my condo to meet Celine and the limo downstairs, I ran into Anna, who was also dressed up. Unlike me, however, she looked thin and glamorous. She also wore some kind of perfume that smelled vaguely familiar.

"Oh. Hello," she said, locking her door.

I answered her cordially, although what I really wanted to do was grab her by the hair and smash her face into the wall.

"Wow, you look fancy tonight," she said, following me down the hallway toward the elevators. "Do you have a date?"

I was about to tell her I didn't, but something came over me. "Yes. I do."

We stopped at the end of the hallway and I pressed the DOWN button.

"How nice for you," she replied.

How *nice* for me? Grr…

"What about you? Are you seeing…" my eye twitched and I could barely get his name out, "Sonny tonight?"

She smiled. "Yes. We're going to see *My Life In Chaos* in concert. I'm meeting him for dinner, first. We have reservations for *The Marble Horse* before the show. "

Her words felt like a hard kick to the gut. I felt physically ill as the memories of canceling the reservations I'd made for Sonny came rushing back to me. If that wasn't bad enough, they were going to the same concert and... I'd lied about having a date. If she saw me alone or with Celine and the others, she'd probably have a good laugh.

"Oh," was all I could say as we stepped onto the elevator. I quickly pushed the button to the Main Level.

"So... what are you and your date doing tonight?"

There was no way in hell that I was going to tell her. With my luck, we'd run into each other, especially if she was trying to find me.

"I'm not sure. It's supposed to be a surprise," I lied.

I suddenly recognized the perfume she was wearing. It was called *Poison* and Sonny had given me a bottle of it last summer as a gift. I'd kept it, but the bottle was going straight into the garbage when I got home. I was just glad I hadn't worn it that evening. I'd tried a new scent that I'd gotten for Christmas from my mother.

When the doors opened, I couldn't get out of the elevator fast enough. Not only was I shaking with rage, but the perfume thing had almost made me cry. I loathed Sonny now more than ever and was determined to have the time of my life, even if it killed me.

"Have fun tonight!" the fake bitch called out.

I wanted to turn around and give her the middle finger, but couldn't bring myself to do it. Instead, I said, "Thanks. I will."

47

Chapter 9

Mason

Z ed, our drummer, grumbled, "Another pre-party. Thrilling," when we were in the limo. There were six of us—Me, Zed, Palmer, Frankie, Chance, and of course, Mack. He'd asked us to drive together, so he could keep an eye on everyone. "Tell me again why we're doing these things? We should be at the stadium already. Getting psyched and ready for the concert."

"You do them because the fans love it and are willing to pay an arm-and-a-leg to catch a glimpse of you. Plus, it's great publicity. Not many artists show up at pre-parties," Mack replied, not looking up from his cell phone.

"Gee, I wonder why," Frankie, our bass player, said dryly.

"It's because it's bullshit, man," Chance said before taking a drag of his e-cigarette. "Why don't they just come to the after-party?"

"Because we've made them private," Mack reminded him. "And more controllable."

Chance laughed. "Oh yeah. I guess the last big one got a little out of hand."

That was an understatement. People had gotten so trashed and rowdy, including some of my bandmates, the cops had been called. Mack had been livid and so had our publicist. Fortunately, I'd already left the party and had missed the show.

"No shit," Mack, who was also his uncle, said. "Also, with our Stalker John problem, I think it's better to just keep the parties small for the time being. At least until he fades away."

"Is he still sending threatening letters?" Zed asked me.

"Probably," I said. "The guy is a flake."

"What's his problem anyway?" Palmer asked.

"His wife left him. Apparently, it's my fault," I replied.

Frankie snorted. "Did you fuck her or something?"

"I've never even met her," I replied. At least not that I knew of.

"Maybe one of us did and he's barking up the wrong tree," said Chance, laughing harder than necessary.

"Are you high?" Mack asked, his eyes narrowing.

His smile fell. "No. I just think it's funny."

"This isn't a laughing matter. This guy is a certifiable whack-job," Mack replied. "You haven't seen his letters. He really wants Mason dead."

I rubbed my eye. "Thanks for reminding me," I mumbled.

"There's a fine line between love and hate. *Maybe*, he's obsessed because he wants you," Chance replied, his sense of humor twisted as usual. "And is jealous that you screwed his wife and not him."

"Number one, get bent. Number two, I know all the chicks I've had sex with, and none of them were married, least of all to Stalker John," I said, although that wasn't entirely true. I'd had sex with a lot of women in the past and the only thing I'd been sure of was that I'd used protection. Another reason why I was trying to abstain from jumping in the sack with just anyone. "Number three, can we change the fucking subject?"

"Yeah. Let's change it," Frankie said, looking bored. "I'd rather talk about the *real* party. The one after the concert. Do we have some extra tickets?"

"I have a few," Mack said, patting his pocket.

"So if we see some bangable chicks here tonight, we can use them?" Chance asked with a smirk.

"Yes, but use them sparingly," he replied and looked at me. "You want some of the passes, too?"

"Nah," I replied.

"Mason, what's going on with you, man? You seeing someone?" Palmer asked.

"No," I replied.

"You *have* been kind of down lately. Everything all right?" Mack asked, eyeing me with concern.

"Everything is fine." I wasn't about to get into it with him or any of the other band members. They lived for the parties and women. All I cared about was the music and that was beginning to wane. Especially since I wasn't allowed to write my own songs anymore. Hell, I couldn't remember the last time I played one of them at a concert.

"Cheer up then. The fans want to see you smiling," Mack said, still trying to get a read on me.

I smirked. "This better?"

"The chicks won't give a shit if he's smiling or glaring at 'em. All they care about is that he's," Frankie raised his voice a few octaves, "Mason Stone."

I couldn't exactly argue that fact. Hell, I could stop taking showers and let myself go for a month and my fame would still draw in the fanatical groupies. Many wouldn't consider smelling like an outhouse a problem, as long as it was me.

"Hey, did anyone see Zondra today?" Chance asked.

Zondra was the lead singer of The Sun Chasers. They were our opening band.

"I talked to her on the phone," I replied. "About an hour ago." She'd called to ask if I was going to the after-party and I told her I wasn't sure. We'd gone out a long time ago, but were just friends now.

"What did she have to say?" Mack asked.

I told him.

"So, you're not going to the after-party?" Chance asked, surprised.

I shrugged.

"The fans expect you to be there," Mack said. "At least make an appearance. Have a couple of drinks and leave."

"Fine. I'm driving separate then," I replied.

"Do what you want. Just be there," he said.

In other words, contradict myself, I thought glumly.

Chapter 10

Terra

The limo was parked right outside of the building. I quickly raced down the steps and the driver let me in.

"You look amazing!" Celine said, after we greeted each other. She was holding a glass of champagne and already grinning from ear-to-ear.

"Thanks. You, too!" I yelled over the music.

"Sorry, I guess this is a little loud." Celine picked up a remote and turned the volume down, and then moved over to give me a hug. After releasing me, she nodded in approval. "I love your hair. It looks like you had your eyebrows done, too."

She didn't miss anything.

"Yeah, I was talked into it," I admitted.

"Whoever did them did a great job," she replied, studying my face.

"Where'd you go?" Celine's sister, Wanda, asked.

I told her about Sebastian and the hair salon.

"The last time I had my eyebrows done, they made them look way too thin," Kira said. "I'm going to use your guy next."

She was right. They looked like there wasn't much left, but she was still a beautiful woman.

I told them that Sebastian used to go to high school with

Mason Stone.

"You're kidding?" Celine said, her eyes wide. "Did he give you any dirt on him?"

I told them what he'd told me.

"From what I've read in the tabloids, he's not like that now," Celine replied. "He's a big partier and has dated quite a few women."

"Ah, the life of a rock star. I guess that doesn't surprise me one bit," Wanda replied.

I nodded. "By the way, you all look great."

Just as I'd suspected, they each had on expensive dresses and were dressed to kill. They were a couple of years apart from each other, but could almost pass for triplets. All three were full-figured, with flawless mocha skin, large hazel eyes, and high, rounded cheekbones. As for their hair, Celine wore hers in braids, Kira's went past her shoulders in thick waves, and Wanda was currently sporting a dyed-blonde bob. They were all very striking.

"Wait a second," Celine said, looking out the window as the driver began pulling away from the curb. She pointed a long, red nail toward Anna. "Isn't that the bitch who stole your man?"

"Yes. Unfortunately," I replied as the other two women gawked at Anna, too.

Celine turned to me with fire in her eyes. "I have a thing or two to say to that tramp." She rolled down the glass that separated us from the driver. "Could you please stop the limo?"

Oh no.

"Sure," he said, putting on the brakes.

"Wait. No, no, no," I said quickly, my gut twisting at the thought. "I told her that I was going on a date. If she sees you, she'll know I was lying."

"Why did you tell her that?" she asked, staring at me like I was crazy.

"I don't know. I guess I didn't want her to think I was pining after Sonny," I replied, ashamed.

"I can't believe he left you for that skinny bitch," Wanda said as we watched Anna walk to her car. "Obviously, he doesn't deserve you anyway, but what in the hell was he thinking? She doesn't even have any boobs. Didn't you say he wouldn't let you get a breast-reduction?"

"He's the damn boob," Celine snapped as I nodded my head.

We laughed.

"Let's forget about that asshole. He's obviously an idiot and you're better off without him. Now, I'm already buzzed and you're not. Let's fix that," Celine said. "By the way, Driver, you can leave now."

"Yes, ma'am," he replied, also chuckling.

Celine turned the music up.

I thought about telling her that Sonny and Anna would be at the concert, but I knew that the odds of us running into them were pretty small, so I didn't.

"The concert isn't for a couple more hours. What are we going to do until then?" I asked instead.

"We're going to a private pre-concert party at *The Legends of Rock Cafe*. Jimmy was able to get us into that, too." Celine handed me an empty glass and then opened up a bottle of champagne. Reaching over, she filled the glass with bubbly.

"I heard that Mr. Super Star might be stopping in quickly before the concert starts, too."

I grinned. "Wow. Jimmy really went all out for you. He's so sweet," I replied, imagining the two of them together. They really were a great couple, although they argued constantly about stupid things. It was their way, though; everyone who knew them knew how much they loved each other. They were destined to grow old together and I was happy for my best friend.

"Yeah. My Jimmy is the best," she replied, topping off her own glass of champagne.

"Amen, to that," Kira said.

Wanda nodded. "Mm-hm. You struck gold with that boy. She chuckled. "Not only is he handsome and sweet, he literally *has* gold-lined pockets. You lucked out with the complete package there, Celine."

Celine frowned. "You know he wasn't rich when I met him. I'm *not* a gold-digger." She set the bottle down and took a sip of her champagne.

"Lord," Wanda shook her head. "There you go again. You gotta quit being so defensive. I didn't mean anything by it other than Jimmy has everything a girl needs, which is hard to find these days. You know what I'm saying?" she said, looking at me.

I nodded.

Did I ever.

"I'm just messing with you," Celine said, smirking. "Of course I know what you meant. Anyway, your man Tyrell is pretty sweet, too. He treats you damn good and you're definitely not living in a shack."

"I know. I know," Wanda said. "I'm not complaining

55

about my life. Just complimenting yours."

"I appreciate it." She looked over at her other sister. "You're not doing so bad for yourself either," Celine said.

"No I'm not. I'll drink to that," Kira replied, raising her glass.

Kira's husband, David, was a doctor. I'd only met him a couple of times, but he seemed like a really nice guy.

We toasted and then the three of them looked at me.

"Now, we just need to find you a man," Celine said, a smile curving on her full lips.

"I had one, and look how that turned out. No thank you," I replied.

"You still need one for sex." Her eyebrow arched. "Unless, you're changing courts?"

"Celine," laughed Kira. "Really?"

She gave her a serious look. "Yeah, *really*. Her mother did. There's no shame in that. Celine looked at me again. "Hell, if you decide you want to, I work with this lesbian who is really nice—"

"I'm *not* gay," I cut in, smiling and shaking my head. I don't know who was worse—my mother or Celine. Both wanted to fix me up. "I would have told you."

"Okay. I'm just putting it out there. Anyway, no matter what you decide, you know I will always love ya, Terrabae," she said.

I stared at her in amusement. "I appreciate that, and I love you, too. But, I have no desire to... you know..."

"Munch carpet?" Kira asked and we all started laughing.

"Exactly. And, I've got enough boobs of my own to be

fascinated by anyone else's," I said, chuckling. "I'll be honest with you, though. I do miss having sex. With *men*," I clarified.

"See? We need to get her *laid*," Celine said, raising her glass. "Another toast! Let's find Terra a man. One with a big—"

"Celine!" Kira gasped. "Really?"

"You didn't let me finish. One with a big *heart!*" she replied, her eyes gleaming wickedly. "And a big… *wallet*."

"And a big ol' dick!" Wanda hollered just as the limo driver turned down the music. Seeing his expression in the rearview mirror, we all lost it.

"Sorry, Fred," Celine said, when she was finished laughing. "What did you need?"

"I forgot to ask where exactly you wanted me to drop you off?" he asked, his eyes smiling.

"*The Legends of Rock Cafe*. Thank you," she replied.

"That's what I thought… but I wanted to make sure. Carry on," he said and then rolled up the privacy glass.

"Did you see his face?" laughed Wanda, wiping the tears from her eyes. "I feel so trashy."

"You know what they say," Kira said. "You can take the girl out of the ghetto—"

"But you can't take the ghetto out of the girl," Celine finished for her, laughing again.

"And so the hell what. We have character, don't we?" Wanda said, her eyes sparkling.

"Excuse me, but… you did *not* grow up in the ghetto," I said with a smirk. "In fact, your parents owned their own business, right?"

They grew up in a great neighborhood, always wore name-brand clothing, and their mother paid for them to have manicures at least twice a month.

"Compared to where we're living now, believe me... it was like the ghetto," Wanda said. "I'm spoiled now. I won't deny it. My man even draws my baths for me in the Jacuzzi. And then *leaves*."

"Really? Damn. You've got it good, Wanda," Kira said. "Don't ever let that one go."

"No doubt," she replied.

"We've all been lucky. That's going to change for you though," Celine said, looking at me.

"I hope so," I replied.

"It will. I can feel it. Now... who wants more? It's time to really get this party started," she said, holding up the bottle.

We all held out our glasses.

❤

I had to admit, I wasn't used to drinking, so by the time we made it to *The Legends of Rock Cafe*, I was bubbly and lightheaded. After getting our passes checked by a bouncer, we stepped into the back room, where the restaurant had sectioned it off for the pre-party.

"Wow, this place is jam-packed," remarked Wanda as we each grabbed a glass of white wine from one of the servers.

"Yeah," I replied, gazing around at the crowd of people. There was quite the mix, too. Some were dressed in tailored suits and designer dresses, while others looked like they'd just stepped off of a country singer's tour bus. It just went to show that the band's fans came from all walks of life. It wasn't surprising, however. They were very talented.

"Do you see Mason Stone anywhere?" Celine asked, looking around.

"No," Wanda replied. "I doubt he's here, otherwise everyone would be surrounding him."

"True." I felt someone bump into me from behind. The place was so crowded it was getting hard to breathe. "Maybe we should find a table?" I suggested.

"Good luck," Kira replied dryly.

I saw some tables on the other side of the room. Unfortunately, the people seated didn't look like they were getting up anytime soon.

Sighing, I took a sip of the wine and found it too bitter to be enjoyable. But it was free and probably a lot less carbs than what I normally enjoyed.

"This wine is too dry," Kira said, puckering her lips and making a face. "I think I'm going to get something else to drink."

"That might take a while," Celine said, motioning toward the crowded bar where several bartenders were racing back and forth to mix drinks. "The lines aren't moving very fast."

Kira sighed. "Wonderful. Well, I guess I can wait."

"I hate to say this, but I have to go to the bathroom," Wanda said. "Does anyone want to come with me?"

"I will," Kira replied. "Do you want my wine, Celine?"

"No," she replied.

Kira looked at me.

"No thanks. I'm with you. The wine is a little too dry. Plus, I'm getting a little tipsy. I probably shouldn't drink too much more."

Celine snorted. "Girl, that's the point. To get tipsy and *stay* tipsy. Besides, you're not driving. Take advantage of it and enjoy yourself."

"Yes, ma'am," I replied smiling.

"Why don't you two stand in line for drinks while we're in the bathroom?" Kira said, looking past us toward the bar.

"Good idea," Celine said. "What do you two want?"

"I'll have a rum and Coke," Kira said, reaching into her purse. She pulled out her wallet and was about grab some cash when Celine stopped her.

"I got this. What about you, Wanda?" she asked.

"I'll take a Mai Tai," she replied.

"Ooh, get me that instead," Kira said. "A Mai Tai sounds delicious right now."

"Yeah, it does. I'm getting one, too. Why don't you two meet us back here?" Celine replied. "Hopefully, we'll get the drinks before the concert starts."

"No doubt," she replied. "We'll see you in a bit. Come on, Wanda."

They left and I followed Celine to the bar. "Keep your eyes out for Mason Stone or one of the other band members," she said, looking at me sideways.

"I'll try," I replied. I had no idea what the other members looked like, but something told me they'd be easy to spot.

As we stood in line for the drinks, a guy in front of us,

who was obviously hammered, turned and stared right at my chest. It didn't help that he was short and they were at eye-level.

"Good, *God*," he said loudly, swaying. "Are those things even *real*?"

People turned to look and I was mortified.

"Excuse me?" Celine said angrily. "Tell me I did *not* hear you just ask her that?"

Blinking, he gave her a sheepish grin. "Sorry. I didn't mean for that to actually come out. I just didn't expect to turn around and see…" he replied, his eyes traveling back to my chest and then my face. "Them. I mean, you."

"It's okay," I answered, wishing I could disappear. "Let's just forget about it."

Celine clucked her tongue. "Not, it is most certainly *not* okay," she said. "You should be ashamed of yourself. In fact, for being such a pig, I think you should pay for our drinks."

He laughed. "You drive a hard bargain. It's an open bar!"

She looked him over with disgust. "Free drinks? No wonder why a cheap-assed drunk like you is here."

Oh, shit.

"Excuse me?" the guy said, looking angry.

"Hey, look. The line looks shorter on the other side. Maybe we should go over there," I said trying to pull her away.

Celine snorted. "Shorter isn't always better. I'm sure his dates would agree."

"Wow. What's your problem? You a feminist or something?" he asked, too drunk and ignorant to know when he's said enough. "I mean, for shit's sake, some women spend thousands of dollars to look like your friend here, and I was just paying her a compliment. Among other things, your attitude is what's wrong with the world today."

"Hold my purse," Celine said, shoving it at me. "I'll show him 'attitude'."

I quickly got between him and Celine. "I appreciate you sticking up for me, but I've got this," I said, staring into her eyes.

She didn't look like she believed me.

"Give me a break. How did you two cows even get invited to this party? Did you flash one of the security guards your jugs?" he asked.

My eye twitched. Even I have my breaking point.

I turned around and my fist connected with his nose. He stumbled backward, falling into a skinny fifty-something cougar wearing leather and tall heels.

"Watch out, you asshole!" she screamed, shoving him away from her.

Regaining his balance, he covered his nose, which was starting to bleed, and stumbled toward me.

Celine pulled out a canister of pepper spray and aimed it at him. "That's right. Come and get it, *asshole*."

He froze. "You two bitches are crazy!"

A bouncer named Steve appeared next to him. "Let's go. You're out of here."

He stared at Steve in disbelief while he held his nose with one hand and pointed at me with the other. "It was her fault!"

"Don't worry. She's leaving, too," said a voice behind me.

My heart sank. I turned around and saw another bouncer, even bigger than the first, named Luke. "I'm sorry. I wasn't thinking."

"Doesn't matter. There's absolutely no fighting in here and those are the rules. You're going to have to leave."

"She didn't do anything," Celine lied.

"We saw her assault him," Luke said.

"She was defending herself," Celine replied in disbelief.

"We didn't see him doing her any bodily harm," a third bouncer said, coming up to us.

"So, if he would have hit her, everything would be okay?" Celine asked angrily.

"Let her stay," said one of the guys standing in line. "He deserved what he got. You should have heard him."

"Yeah. He was a dickhead," replied his friend.

Their support was appreciated, but it didn't change the bouncers' minds. They walked me to the front door as Celine reluctantly went in search of Wanda and Kira. As I was about to leave the building, the front door opened and in walked a group of security guards ushering people out of the way. Behind them, dressed in low-riding jeans, a long-sleeved dark-blue shirt, and leather vest, was the legend himself — Mason Stone.

My jaw hit the floor as I got a closer look.

It was *him*.

The guy from the bakery.

Chapter 11

Mason

I did a double-take when I walked in and saw Terra, and what a vision she was. Tonight she had on a dress that showed off her sexy legs and it looked like she's spent a lot of time on her hair and makeup. What really got me were those eyes of hers, though. Piercing green eyes that reminded me of a cat's.

"Hello there, Sweet Cakes," I said, still shocked that the one person I couldn't stop thinking about was standing right in front of me. What were the odds of that?

She stared at me wide-eyed, looking just as surprised as me. "It's, um, *Sweet Treats*. The bakery is actually called Sweet *Treats...*"

"I guess I just still have your cakes on my mind," I replied with a smile.

Terra blushed and I realized where her mind may have gone. Just like earlier when I'd mentioned the muffins.

A dirty-minded woman.

I kind of liked that.

My eyes dipped down to her soft curves, which my palms ached to explore. Although the sequined jacket covered most of her chest, her dress revealed an ample amount of cleavage. Enough to get lost in for a week.

"The party is in the back," Jack, one of our security guards said. "We should hurry."

"Yeah. I know. Hold on," I replied, wanting to explain

things to Terra. I imagined that she was pissed off I'd lied —
and wouldn't blame her if she was. Before I could say
anything, some muscle-head bouncer named Steve touched
her elbow, making her flinch.

She glared at him and shook her arm away. "Don't touch
me."

"Time to leave," he replied gruffly.

"What's going on?" I asked.

"She assaulted someone," Steve explained.

I raised my eyebrow and stared at him in disbelief.

Terra

I groaned in the back of my throat. The bouncer was making
me sound like a freaking crazy woman.

"I hit this jerk back there because he insulted me and my
friend. *Several* times. I don't usually get into fights but, I can
honestly say that he had it coming," I explained, trying to
keep my cool.

Mason turned back to the bouncer. "Sounds like he
deserved whatever he got. I think you should let her back
in."

I could tell the bouncer wanted to tell him where to go,
but instead he relented and walked away.

Relieved, I smiled at Mason. "Thank you."

"No problem." His eyes swept over me. "You clean up
very nicely, by the way. I almost didn't recognize you

without your uniform on."

Pleased, I could feel myself blushing again. "Thank you."

"Sorry, I lied, by the way," he said, lowering his voice and looking around. "I was playing hooky and wasn't supposed to be wandering the streets. My manager would kill me if he found out about it."

"It's okay. I totally understand." And I did. I couldn't even imagine what his life was like. He probably didn't have a moment of peace when he was out in public.

"Mason, we need to get moving or we'll be late for the show," said one of the other guys from the band.

"I know," he replied and looked at me again. "Walk in with me?"

My eyes widened. "Really?"

"Yeah. I wouldn't want anyone else to try and kick you out," he said with a smile. "If you're at my side, they wouldn't dare."

I laughed nervously. "Right."

He grabbed my hand and slid it through the crook of his arm. "Ready?"

Suddenly feeling anxious, I could only nod. Here I was, on the arm of a hot and famous celebrity. Now that I knew who he really was, my knees felt wobbly and my stomach was doing flip-flops. Yeah, he seemed down-to-earth and nothing like I would have expected, but he was still *Mason Stone*. A man, larger-than-life. Someone who was idolized by millions of people. It was hard to believe that I was actually on his arm at that moment.

"Hey, Mason. Who is this?" one of the other guys from the band asked. He had short, spiky blonde hair, a goatee, and a multitude of tattoos and piercings. Kind of cute if you were into rough-looking bad boys.

"Terra," he replied without further comment.

"Okay, then. Well, I'm Zed, that's Palmer, Frankie, and Chance," he said, waving his thumb at their other bandmates, who were all staring at me curiously.

"Nice to meet you," I replied, glancing at the others quickly. I'd seen them on television and in magazines, but Mason had been the one who'd stood out for me. Seeing them in person, I noticed that they were all pretty good-looking in their own ways.

"So, you two old buds?" Zed asked as we headed back toward the party.

"Something like that. I'll explain later," Mason told him.

"You don't have to explain anything." Zed smiled at me. "You coming to the after-party?"

I was going to tell him 'no' when Mason confirmed that I was.

"I don't think I can. I'm with some friends," I said, flattered that he wanted me there.

"Any of them your date?" he asked.

I snorted. "No. No dates."

He grinned. "Then no worries. Your friends are invited, too. I'll get you some passes after we take care of this," Mason said.

I grinned. "Wow, okay. Thank you," I replied, imagining how excited Celine and the others were going to be when I told them.

He winked. "My pleasure."

When we entered the party, the crowd went crazy. We were quickly surrounded by excited fans, who were either holding up their cell phones for pictures or trying to touch one of the band members. As the security guards ushered us toward a stage that had been set up, I heard my name. It was Celine and her sisters. All three looked stunned to see me with Mason.

I gave them a helpless grin and shrugged.

Smiling, Celine held up her phone and took some pictures. Meanwhile, Mason still had his hand on my arm possessively. It felt like I was in a dream.

"Mason!" screamed fans. "Over here!"

"We love you!" others screamed.

As we walked the rest of the way to the stage, the crowd kept trying to get closer, and even though I wasn't even a member of the band, it was quite nerve-wracking.

"Crazy, huh?" he said near my ear.

I shuddered at his breath on me. "Yeah. A little bit."

When we finally reached the stage, Mason released my hand. "Just in case we get separated, I'll have my manager, Mack, give you those passes," he said loudly. "How many will you need?"

"There's four of us. Thank you again!" I replied.

"No problem." He looked over my head. "Mack!"

I turned to see a man in a dark gray suit moving toward us.

"Get her four after-party passes," he instructed as Mack

68

stopped next to us.

His manager, a heavyset man with a moustache, reached into his pocket, and handed four cards to me. "I guess you changed your mind?"

"Guess I did." Mason looked at me again and smiled. "See you soon, Sweet Cakes."

Star-struck, all I could do was smile back. As far as I was concerned, he could call me whatever he wanted.

Mason got up onstage with the others and Celine managed to catch up to me.

"Now how in the hell did that happen?" she asked, looking flabbergasted.

I went over it quickly.

Kira gasped. "You had Mason Stone in your bakery and didn't tell us?"

"I didn't know, I swear! Although Cindy pretty much asked him if he was Mason Stone and he kind of denied it. I guess," I replied, thinking back to the conversation. "He obviously lied, but... I get why."

"I would too if I was him," Celine said. "If anyone knew that Mason Stone was walking around Minneapolis, there'd have been a stampede of fans."

"Definitely. Oh, and guess what?" I said, smiling.

"What?" Celine asked.

I showed them the tickets to the *My Life In Chaos After-Party* and they all shrieked.

"Girl, I think he's hot for you," Celine said, winking at me.

"Right. I *don't* think so," I replied, although I felt a warm rush of pleasure at the crazy notion.

"He *was* holding on to you like he was afraid you were going to get away," Wanda said.

Kira nodded in agreement. "Mm...hmm..."

Before I could reply, Mason asked for everyone's attention. The crowd quieted down and he began to speak.

"First of all, I just want to say how much I *love* Minneapolis!" Mason called out.

The crowd clapped and roared with approval. When they eventually quieted down, he talked about growing up in Minnesota and how it was his favorite place to tour. After a few more words, he handed the mic over to the other band members, who each addressed the fans. Finally, they took some questions, thanked everyone for coming, and then apologized for having to run.

"Thanks for coming and we'll see you all at the concert!" Mason called out before they were ushered off stage and back through the crowd once more. Unfortunately, everyone kept pushing and shoving, so we couldn't get close to them again, but I didn't care. I was too excited thinking about not only the concert, but the *after-party*. I still couldn't believe we were invited. And by Mason himself.

Good God, what if he really was attracted to me?

Being the rock star that he was, he probably expected to get laid later. I pictured the two of us in bed and heat filled my belly.

"What's going through your head right now?" Celine asked as we left the restaurant.

I wiped the stupid grin off my face. "Nothing. Why?"

"She was obviously thinking about Mr. Super Star," Kira

said. "I know I'd be thinking about him. Thinking about that hot body on top of mine."

I gasped and chuckled. "You would."

"When was the last time you had sex?" Celine asked. "Don't tell me it was with Sonny."

"Okay, I won't tell you," I replied, the idea depressing even to myself. But sex wasn't something I gave away lightly. I'd never have a one night stand, even with Mason Stone. It was hard enough taking my clothes off for myself, let alone a perfect stranger. I was a modest woman, and at the moment, definitely comfortable in my own skin.

"She shouldn't have sex with him," Wanda told the other two as the limo driver pulled up. "Imagine how many women he's been with or will be with, tonight alone."

"Like there is even a chance of that," I said, laughing dryly. "Mason Stone is not looking to have sex with me."

"Then why did he invite you to his after-party?" Celine asked.

"For my… cake. He's just being nice because he wants a birthday cake," I said as the limo driver opened up the back door to let us in.

"Served in her birthday suit," Kira said with a wicked gleam in her eye.

"You know that's right," Celine said, laughing and giving her a high-five.

"You have it all wrong," I said lightly as I followed them into the vehicle. "You'll see."

And if they were right, Lord help me.

Chapter 12

Mason

"S o… spill beans. Who was the chick back there?" Chance asked on the way to the stadium.

"Just someone I know. Nobody special," I replied, not wanting to get into it with Mack sitting there.

"If she's nobody special then you won't mind if I have a go with her, right?" Palmer asked with a lascivious smile. "You know how I like my women, and she's got it all… and more."

"You like your women any way you can get 'em," I replied dryly. "And yeah, I do mind. She's a friend."

"With benefits?" Chance asked. "If so, I could use a new friend."

The others laughed.

I shook my head.

"Quit giving him shit. He's finally got a smile on his face," Mack replied. "Let him have some fun."

"She was sure smiling," Chance said. "Friends or not, she's star-struck and probably willing to get on her knees before the night is over."

"You're such an asshole," I muttered.

"A jealous one," added Frankie.

"I'm not jealous of anyone," Chance said angrily. "Fuck you."

"Chill the hell out," Mack said with a pained look. "This is no time to argue. You're going to be on stage soon performing. There's no time for this shit."

Nobody said anything.

Sighing, I stared outside as the limo continued on its way, thinking about what Chance had said. Was Terra starstruck? That's not what I'd wanted. She knew who I was now, but I had no idea who she was or if she had scruples. I decided that if anything, it was certainly worth checking out.

♥

Terra

The concert was unforgettably amazing, although we almost missed the opening band, The Sun Catchers. I'd never heard of them, but the lead singer's name was Zondra, and her voice was sultry, rich, and absolutely beautiful. I'd have paid to see her even without Mason's band, she was just *that* talented.

After returning for an encore, The Sun Catchers gave up the stage for Mason's band around nine-thirty. Of course, they put on a phenomenal show. Not only did he sound absolutely amazing *live,* but the light show and special effects brought it all together. By the end of the concert, my voice was gone, my hands were tired from clapping, and my cheeks ached from smiling so much. It was the best performance I'd ever seen. Admittedly, I'd only been to a handful of concerts nor had I ever met the musicians personally, but there was no denying why Mason filled every seat in the stadium.

"That was unbelievable," Celine said, as we headed toward the stage with our backstage passes in hand. "Probably one of the best concerts I've ever seen."

"It was pretty good, even for rock," Wanda said. "I'm usually more into hip-hop, but that was entertaining. Especially when the drummer did that long solo while Mason changed costumes."

"Yeah, he's really good," I replied, thinking back to that moment Mason had left the stage, returning in what looked like black leather pants and a matching jacket with nothing underneath but muscle and tattoos.

"He must have gotten so hot and sweaty, running around with that guitar of his and singing like he did," Kira said. "He really worked his ass off on that stage. I hope he has time to take a shower before going to his party."

Celine laughed. "Only you would think about that. Anyway, I'd be willing to bet that some of his fans would happily lick every ounce of sweat from his body, showered or not."

"Oh, I'm sure," she replied. "There are some nasty bitches out there."

When we finally found our way to the entrance to the backstage, we were one of the last to arrive and there was a long line ahead of us.

"Damn, I hope this line moves fast," Wanda said, yawning. "I mean, it's already getting late and we still have that after-party to go to." She looked at me and smiled. "Unless, you just want to skip it."

"Hell no," Celine answered for me. "That's not going to happen. I don't care if we're out all night, we're going to that party. We might never have a chance like this again, and

Terra might not ever have another shot at Mason."

"Will you *stop*?" I said, flabbergasted. Just looking at the other women waiting to get backstage, some looking like they'd just stepped out of a Victoria's Secret commercial, I knew it was a ridiculous idea. "I'm not 'getting' with anyone."

"Yeah. We'll see," she replied, a determined look on her face.

It was obvious she was on a mission, and knowing Celine, she was going to do everything in her power to try and get us together. It was a lost cause and a potentially embarrassing situation.

"Celine." I touched her arm. "Look at me and look at… women like that," I said, nodding toward two gals ahead of us who were gorgeous and skinny. "There's not a chance in hell that he's going to want someone like me when he has women like that falling at his feet. So, please, just let it go."

Her eyes grew soft. "You really don't know how beautiful you are, do you?"

Flattered, I sighed. "I love you, you know that?"

She touched my face and smiled affectionately. "I love you, too. Which is why I think you deserve the best."

"And the best is a one-night stand with Mason Stone?" I asked, incredulous.

She shrugged. "Maybe for tonight it is. You're obviously attracted to the man. Hell, you're a grown woman anyway. What's the harm in having a little fun?"

"One-night stands are not my idea of fun."

"You've never had one so how do you know they're not?" she replied.

I didn't reply.

"Girl, chances like this don't come around often. Don't give me that look. I saw the way you were looking at him," she said. "You're attracted to the man."

She was right. The truth was, the more I thought of it, if the man actually *did* make a move, I didn't know if I'd turn him down. Especially after watching him on stage. It had been one of the sexiest things I'd ever seen. Watching those hips move to the music, and listening to him pour his heart out in the songs, had started a wildfire in my panties.

"I'll tell you something else, if you think he gave you these passes because of your cakes, you're crazy. He wants more than that."

I sighed. It was like talking to a wall. "Yeah, well we'll see."

She gave me one of her *I know I'm right* looks. "Yeah. We will."

By the time we finally made it backstage, my feet were killing me from the high heels and I was getting weary.

"Hey, long time no see," Zed said, grinning at us from behind a roped-in area surrounded by their security team.

"I know, right?" I replied, smiling back. Looking around, I didn't see Mason and wondered where he was.

Palmer, Frankie, and Chance also greeted us warmly.

"Sweet Cakes," Mason said, stepping out of the back with a devilish grin. I noticed he'd changed again, this time into a pair of faded blue jeans and the same black concert T-shirt I'd managed to purchase right before the concert.

"Sweet *Treats*," I corrected.

Smiling, he took a swig from the water bottle he held and then asked if we'd enjoyed the concert.

"It was amazing," Celine gushed. "You guys hit it out of the ballpark. It had to be the best concert I'd ever seen. *All* of us. Especially Terra," she said, looping her arm through mine. "She just couldn't stop talking about it."

"Is that right?" he asked me with a little smile.

"It *was* really good," I replied, amused. "We loved it."

"Good," he answered, screwing the cap back onto his water bottle. "Where were your seats?"

"We were on main floor, but in the very back," I replied.

"Ah. I tried searching for you in the crowd." Mason smiled again. "Obviously, it was like looking for a needle in a haystack."

Flattered to find that he'd actually been searching for me, I felt my cheeks heat as I smiled back. "I'm sure. How many concerts do you have left in this tour?"

"Three," he replied. "Our next one is in New York. Friday night."

We talked some more about the band's upcoming venues while he and the others autographed our backstage passes. Afterward, we were allowed to take a few selfies with each of them. Celine took one of me and Mason. When he put his arm over my shoulder and drew me in closer, I began to tremble.

"Cold?" he asked, rubbing his thumb on my jacket.

More like hot-and-bothered. "No," I laughed, not cold."

"By the way, you smell great," he murmured near my ear before releasing me.

"Thanks," I replied, shuddering again.

Admittedly, he smelled pretty damn good himself, especially for someone who'd been so active on stage.

Maybe the man didn't sweat?

His scent was woodsy with a hint of citrus. It was enough to make me want to linger under his arm all night. Or find out what he wore and buy a bottle of it myself to sniff when I wanted to remember the night.

"There are only a few people left in line," his manager, Mack, said, walking up to us. "We should wrap this up quickly so you can get to the party."

"Yeah, definitely." Mason looked back at me. "You four are still going, right?"

"I'm not sure," I replied. "It's getting kind of late."

"Hell *yes*, we're going," Celine said, giving me a harsh look before smiling at him. "Where is it being held?"

"It's at Raze Night Club," he replied.

"That place is huge. I've been there before. Are you expecting a big turnout?" Celine asked.

"Not too many. This one's not open to the public. Another reason why we stopped in at the pre-concert party. This is just for the stage-crew and other employees. There will be a handful of fans, I'm sure. But, nothing too crazy," Mason replied.

"Sounds great," Celine said, pulling her purse over her shoulder. "We'll see you there."

"I hope so," Mason replied, winking at me before taking another sip of water.

Smiling again, I waved goodbye as security ushered us toward the exit.

"Hey, hold up," Mason said loudly.

We turned around.

He stepped around the ropes and asked if he could talk to me alone for a second.

Surprised, I nodded, wondering what was going on.

He pulled me aside and asked if I wanted to ride with him to the party.

I blinked. "Me? Why?"

"I thought we could talk about my cake," he replied, his eyes twinkling.

From the way he was looking at me, I thought he might be kidding about the cake, but I wasn't sure. "Really?"

"Yeah. It'll be quiet in the limo. Unlike the party, which will be loud and harder to communicate."

Wow, the man really was serious about his cake.

"Uh, yeah. Sure. I'll ride with you. When are you leaving?" I asked him.

"Soon. I just need to stop at the hotel, take a quick shower, and then we can leave," he replied, pulling out his cell phone.

So, I was going back to his hotel with him?

I wasn't sure how I felt about that. Before I could come up with an excuse not to go, Mason hollered out to Celine that I was riding to the party with him.

A huge grin spread across her face. "Okay. Girl, we'll see you there. Have fun!"

Before I could say anything, Celine and her sisters took off quickly, almost as if they had been expecting me to.

"Mason, we have more coming in," Mack said.

Nodding, he looked at me. "If you're hungry, help yourself to the spread over there," Mason said, motioning toward a table filled with everything from sandwiches to chicken wings.

"I'm good. Thank you," I replied, although my stomach was growling at the sight of the buffet. Nobody else seemed to be eating, however, and I certainly didn't want to be the only one, so I decided against it.

"Okay. Well, feel free to sit down and relax. This shouldn't take too long."

"Sure."

I walked over to the metal chairs set up in the corner and sat down just as the next group was chauffeured in. I watched as he and his bandmates signed autographs, and felt a surge of jealousy when one of the fans, a woman in her forties, asked Mason if she could touch his abs.

"My abs?" he asked, looking amused.

"Yeah. I saw a picture of you with your shirt off and you look so ripped and sexy," she purred and then bit her lower lip. "I just want to see if you're as hard as you look in the magazines."

The rest of the band laughed and started giving him shit.

"I'm sorry. I didn't mean to embarrass you," she said, smiling.

"I'm not embarrassed," he replied and then told her if she

wanted to touch his abs, he was fine with it.

She let out an excited gasp and then placed her hand on his stomach. "Oh, my God, you really are ripped," the woman purred, running her fingers up and down his stomach and chest. "So tell me, how do you feel about older women?"

His bandmates lost it again. Mason just smiled and shook his head.

"I'm sorry. I'm bad. I couldn't resist," the woman said, laughing herself. "I'm sure you have young, beautiful women hitting on you all the time. But, if you ever want an experienced one who knows how to please a man, call me. My name is Lucy and I own Elegant Jewelry up the road. You might not remember my name, but I hope you'll remember my shop."

She sounded like a damn commercial...

"Lucy, you're very sweet and it was nice meeting you," Mason replied, casually removing her hand from his stomach and then shaking it. "I'm so glad you enjoyed the concert."

"It was fabulous," she replied.

"Time's up, ladies," Mack said. "Sorry."

After a chorus of groans, they said their farewells, and then after a couple more fans met with the band, it was time to leave.

"Are you ready?" he asked as the stage crew launched into a flurry of activity around us.

"Uh, sure," I said, barely standing up before my chair was taken and stacked with the others. It was obvious the clean-up crew was on a mission to get everything taken down as quickly and as efficiently as possible.

Noticing, Mason apologized. "As you can imagine, disassembling the stage equipment and props can be a long process. They're used to hustling."

"No apologies needed," I replied. "I don't blame them. I'd want to get out of here too."

"Shall we?" he asked, holding out his hand.

I stared at it, wondering if I'd made a terrible mistake. I was about to go back to this man's hotel room. He was going to take a shower while I waited.

What if he walked out of the bathroom naked?

I wasn't sure what I was getting myself into, but it was too late to back out now...

Chapter 13

Mason

T erra looked uncertain as she took my hand and I wondered what was going through her head. If she knew what was going on in mine, she'd probably be pretty pissed off. The truth was, I'd decided to find out what kind of woman Terra really was—someone with scruples, or a woman willing to spread her legs for a quick romp with the famous Mason Stone. I hoped it wasn't the latter. I wanted a challenge. I wanted a woman with morals and dignity. Of course, I could just date other celebrities—and I had been out with quite a few. Unfortunately, most of the ones I'd gone out with had turned out to be snobs and divas. One woman, an actress, had gotten pissed off when I asked her to leave her Chihuahua at home on our first date. Another woman, a country singer, didn't stop talking about herself or her career. Hell, I couldn't get a word in edgewise throughout the entire date. Finally, I tried dating a supermodel and it turned out all she wanted to do was get high and have sex all night long. I was all for the sex, but the drugs had been a real turnoff. Seeing what substance abuse had done to my old man, I just couldn't watch her snort coke without getting disgusted by it. When I asked her to put the shit away, she freaked out and stormed out of my hotel room. It seemed like I was cursed when it came to women… and it was getting old. I wanted someone down-to-earth, intelligent, and morally driven. An independent woman who wouldn't fall at my feet like I was some kind of god. I wanted a woman who was… unpredictable, but in a good way. I only hoped I wasn't wasting my time. I'd been doing too much of that already.

Terra

Mason's security team escorted us to his limo, which was a very impressive white Hummer H2. The chauffer let us in, and we were alone for the first time, which felt both odd and exciting at the same time.

"Wow, this is huge," I said, looking around the vehicle. There seemed to be enough seating for at least sixteen people.

"Yeah. Mack rents us the larger ones, just in case we need the extra room for guests," he said, sitting across from the mini bar. He held up a bottle of Cristal champagne. "Would you like some?"

I knew drinking around him probably wasn't such a great idea, but I'd never tried Cristal; it was too expensive for my budget. Plus, I had a slight headache and thought a little 'Hair of the Dog' might be just what I needed.

Deciding that one glass couldn't get me into too much trouble, I set my purse down. "Sure. What about you? Are you going to have any?"

"Nah. I'm more of a beer guy," he replied, removing the foil around the top of the bottle.

"Wait, you don't have to open that just for me."

"Nonsense," he replied, smiling. "I want you to enjoy yourself. I'm going to. Especially now that I can relax for a while."

"But—"

"No buts. You're my guest and this stuff is paid for already. May as well enjoy the champagne and not let it go to waste," he replied.

I chuckled. "Okay. Thank you."

"You're welcome."

I watched as he finished opening the bottle and then poured me a large glass.

"Oh, wow," I said as he handed it to me. "You're not trying to get me drunk, are you?"

"Not drunk. Just pleasantly… comfortable," he replied, winking.

"There's that wink again," I said, thinking out loud. I could feel my cheeks turn red and cursed myself inwardly. He probably just winked a lot and I was acting like it was something special just for me.

In reply, Mason grinned.

"So, have you tried this champagne before?" I asked, changing the subject.

"Yeah. It's good. Very good. But, like I said… I'm a beer guy," he replied, grabbing a bottle of Samuel Adams from the ice bucket and opening it. He moved closer to me and held it up. "Shall we toast?"

I raised my glass. "Sure."

"To another concert down, which brings me another day closer to the end of the tour," he replied with a weary smile. "Thank God."

Imagining how exhausting it must be, I nodded. "I'll drink to that."

"Also…a toast to new friends," he added, before clinking

my glass, his gaze never leaving mine.

I laughed nervously. "Yes. Definitely. To new friends."

I took a sip of the champagne, and he'd been right. It was delicious. Definitely the best I'd ever tried. Or maybe I just thought it was because of the price tag and the fact that I was sipping it in a limo with Mason Stone.

"So," he said, studying me carefully. "What brought you to the concert? Are you a die-hard fan, or was it just something to do on a Saturday night?"

I told him about it being Celine's birthday present. "So, her husband gave her the tickets."

"You wouldn't have purchased them yourself?"

Not wanting to lie, I told him I wasn't much for concerts. "I think you have a great voice, though. I enjoy listening to you on the radio."

"What's your favorite song?" he asked, looking amused.

For some reason, my tired brain couldn't come up with a title. "It's that one...crap." I started singing some of the words and he chuckled.

"I think you sing it better than I do," he said softly.

I laughed. "Right."

"To be honest, I'm not a fan."

"Are you talking about my voice or your song?

He chuckled. "Of my music. Not the new stuff, at least."

"Really? Why is that?"

Mason explained that before he'd become famous, he'd written most of his own music and lyrics. "Now, it's out of my hands. All of our songs are created for us. It's pretty lame, actually," Mason said, a pained expression on his face.

"Especially since I have so many new songs rolling around in my head."

"Can't you tell them you want to play your own music?"

"I've tried. The problem is that the songs they've written for us have become chartbusters. Our agents and record producers aren't interested in giving me back the reins." He sighed. "It's all about the money to them. I get it, but it's frustrating."

"What if you just played one of your songs at a concert and see how the crowd reacts?" I replied.

"I've actually thought about doing just that. The others aren't on board with it, though."

"Your band members?"

He nodded.

I sighed. "Screw them. You know how to play the guitar and piano, maybe you should just slip one in sometime?"

Mason looked amused. "Slip one in?"

"Yeah," I sat up straighter. "I mean, you have oodles of talent. I bet your fans would love it."

"I wish it were that easy. Hell, I wish I had the guts to do it."

"You should really consider it. You said so yourself that you used to write your own songs. Those songs were good enough to get you signed on by a record producer, right?"

"Yeah."

"And, you're not happy right now, from what I'm hearing. So, I think you should go for it. I mean, what are they going to do? You're the star of the show. Your band is excellent, but... everyone is there to see *you*, Mason. They want songs they think *you've* written. Songs that have come from your heart."

He sighed.

"I have to be honest, now that I know you didn't write what we were listening to tonight, I'm *very* anxious to hear your stuff," I replied.

I could see by the wistful expression on his face that he was definitely considering the idea.

"You would, huh?"

"Yeah. Of course."

He took another swig of his beer. "Maybe a few more of these and I'll get the courage up."

"Right. Like you need any courage to sing. I saw you onstage. You owned it and everyone watching you," I replied.

"Maybe, but again... it wasn't my music. What if my manager and the producers are right? Maybe my stuff isn't what I think it is anymore," he murmured, peeling the label off of his bottle.

It shocked me that he seemed so confident onstage and yet, his ego wasn't at all what I would have guessed it to be. "Let your fans decide."

He looked up.

"Test me with it. I'll give you my honest opinion," I said, although I wondered now if I would be too biased. The more time I spent with him, the more I was beginning to really like the man. Especially since he was opening up so much.

"I'll try singing loudly when I'm in the shower. How about that?" he said with a teasing smile.

Picturing how sexy that might look, I realized the champagne was already getting to me.

"Okay. So," I replied, sitting back again in the seat. "About that cake…"

The expression on his face made my heart skip a beat.

"Do you, um, have some ideas on decoration?" I prodded, wondering if I'd been wrong about everything. *Was* I there for more than cake talk?

"I have some ideas. I'm just not sure how you're going to feel about them," he replied softly.

"It doesn't matter how *I* feel," I said, pretending as if we were still talking about cake. "As long as you're happy with the results."

His lip twitched. "I'm sorry."

"About what?"

He gave me a disarming smile. "Do you really think I invited you here to just talk about cake?"

I stiffened up.

And there it was.

I didn't know whether to be angry or flattered. I wasn't that type of woman, no matter how sexy the man was.

I took a big gulp of the champagne, trying to think of a comeback. One that would be sassy and smart.

"Terra." He reached his hand over and touched my hair, his bedroom eyes making my pulse rise. "I've been wanting to do this all night. It's even softer than I'd imagined."

"Well, I just had it cut. No more split ends," I said, laughing nervously.

His knuckles brushed against my neck and I jerked back

slightly.

"Speaking of hair, I almost forgot to tell you, I ran into this guy you went to high school with." I rambled on about Sebastian and how I'd met him.

Mason set his beer down and took my champagne. Before I knew it, he was pulling me into his arms.

I stiffened up. "Wait," I said, leaning away from him.

This was wrong. All wrong. This was not my thing and I couldn't imagine how people hooked up so easily on *Tinder*.

His blue eyes pierced mine. "Don't you want this?"

"Whatever gave you that idea?"

"Because you agreed to go back to my hotel room."

"You said you needed to take a shower and... talk about your cake," I said, getting angry.

His eyebrow raised. "You really thought this was just about the cake?"

My eye twitched. "Yeah. Of course."

"So, you *don't* want to have sex with me?"

That had nothing to do with it. I just didn't want to feel like a cheap whore. He could have at least bought me dinner. "When did the words 'fucking' and 'cake' become interchangeable?"

He started to laugh.

"It wasn't meant to be funny."

He laughed harder.

My disappointment in him continued to grow. I'd actually thought that maybe he was better than this. "You're an asshole. I don't care who you are, I'm not interested in

90

having sex with you. Most guys would have at least taken me to a restaurant before making a move like this."

He stopped laughing and cocked an eyebrow. "Are you hungry?"

I wanted to punch him. "No! Tell your driver to let me off somewhere. I'm not impressed with your glam and I don't care that you're famous. I'm not spending another minute with someone like you." I grabbed my phone to text Celine. I would have to think that even she would be irritated by this.

"Terra, hold on," he said, his voice becoming serious. "Please. Look at me."

"What?" I snapped.

"I'm sorry. You're right... I *was* being an asshole. I was testing you."

"*What?!*"

"It's how I weed out the kind of women I'd rather not waste any time with."

His words didn't make a whole lot of sense to me. "You call that weeding out? Has the world gone completely nuts, or is it just me — or should I say *you*?"

Mason's lip twitched. "Let me explain. I'm nothing more than a fantasy to most of women. Or, a conquest. Don't even get me started on the gold-diggers." He sighed. "I just want to be a normal guy who isn't 'Mason Stone' the rock star. I don't want women throwing themselves at me. I *want* to have to work for it."

"Like you were doing a few seconds ago?" I replied, incredulous. "Trying to *work* for it?"

With a pained expression, he rubbed the side of his face. "What I'm trying to say is that from the first moment I laid eyes on you, I was intrigued. It's why I headed back to the bakery in the first place. When I found out you'd left, I was really disappointed."

Was this more bullshit?

"When I saw you tonight, I felt like it was some kind of, I don't know, sign?" His expression was serious. "Honestly, I've never felt this drawn to anyone before. And believe me, I've met thousands of women. But none of them have really stood out like you."

"So, you decided to test me?"

He nodded. "I'm really sorry. From your angle, it probably seemed very shitty. I just had to find out if you were like all the rest. You're obviously not. You're a woman with scruples and class, and I respect the hell out of that."

"What is it you want from me?" I asked, flattered, yet afraid to trust him.

His smile was humorless. "Honestly, I haven't exactly figured it out yet."

We stared at each other for a few seconds and then I broke the silence.

"Well, I'm still not going to have sex with you," I said flatly.

Not tonight, anyway.

"Thank God."

"I don't know if I should be offended by that reply or flattered," I said, relaxing slightly.

His face turned serious. "Let me just get one thing straight… I want you. *Badly*. Now more than ever," he added. "And it's because you're not like all the others."

"Because I have morals?"

"Exactly. That's a hard trait to find when you're in my position. That being said, I was hoping you might want to spend some time together before I leave for New York. Out of bed, of course."

"I don't know. It depends on how busy my schedule is," I replied with a small smile. "I might be able to fit you in between cake and donuts on Monday."

"Please see what you can do."

We stared at each other silently for a few seconds.

"I noticed that you never asked if I was in a relationship."

"Are you?" he asked.

"No."

"I didn't think so."

I frowned. "Really? Why is that?"

"As I said before, you're obviously a woman with integrity. You would have said something before I tried kissing you."

I relaxed. "I'm also a woman who doesn't like to be lied to. If you really do want to hang out with me, remember that. No more testing or games."

He quickly crossed his heart. "I promise."

Chapter 14

Terra

Mason's hotel, the Gingham, was only four blocks away from my shop, which was apparently how he discovered it.

"I slipped out and went for a jog. When I was returning, I decided to check out your bakery," he explained as the limo pulled up to the hotel. "I have a sweet-tooth like you wouldn't believe."

"Did you ever get that donut?"

He smiled. "I bought four Long Johns when I went back, looking for you."

I stared at him. It was hard to believe he was attracted to a woman like me. I wondered if it was because he'd been with so many skinny ones and wanted to try something new.

"What is it?" he asked.

"Nothing," I replied.

He finished his beer. "You're still unsure of me."

"Of course."

"Don't be. Under all of this... *glam*," he said, repeating me, "I'm just a regular guy who wants what everyone wants—a real, genuine relationship not built on fortune or fame."

I raised my eyebrow. "You're looking for a relationship?"

"Honestly, I'm just looking for something nice. Something *real*. Something I haven't had for a very long time."

94

Before I could reply, the limo driver opened the door and let us out.

"What a relief," Mason said, looking around. "No mobs."

Just his security guards, who'd followed us in another vehicle. They accompanied us into the hotel and up to his suite, which was on the top floor.

"That must get old," I said when we were alone.

"You have no idea," he replied. "Mack's security follows me everywhere. I had to sneak out to go jogging by myself. I can't stand when they shadow me."

"So, they send someone out jogging with you?" I asked, amused.

He nodded. "Either that or they follow me in a car."

"Wow. So, were they angry when you returned by yourself the other day?"

"They didn't actually know I was gone."

A security guard opened the suite door, and after looking around, ushered us in and closed the door behind us.

I immediately took off my heels and resisted a groan, as the plush, beige carpeting felt luxurious under my sore feet. I wasn't used to wearing heels and now remembered why I usually steered clear of them.

"This place is amazing," I said, walking toward the large floor-to-ceiling windows. They provided a panoramic view of the city lights below. It was absolutely breathtaking, especially since we were up so high.

"Yeah, it's a far cry from when we first started touring five years ago," he said. "We shared rooms and sometimes, there were unwanted guests already living in the mattresses."

I shuddered. "Gross."

He chuckled. "Hell yeah it was. Even now I still check the beds, even in places like this. That's one thing you'll find about me; I have a touch of O.C.D. when it comes to my hotel rooms."

"I don't blame you."

"Make yourself at home. I'm going to jump in the shower."

I turned around and noticed he'd taken off shirt, revealing several tattoos and a body that made my throat go dry. I could now see why the woman from earlier wanted to touch him. Mason was muscular, lean, and sexier than anyone had a right to be.

Maybe I was being a little hasty earlier. Sex with him might be worth a little guilt...

"Okay," I said, watching as he disappeared into the back bedroom.

"There's refreshments in the refrigerator," he called. "Help yourself!"

"Thanks!"

Not thirsty, I walked over to the white leather sectional and sat down. Across from me was a piano and some sheet music. I stood up and took a closer look. The notes appeared to be sketched in with a pencil.

His songs, I thought, picturing Mason there, playing and writing down ideas.

Suddenly, my phone went off. I dug it out of my purse and noticed it was Celine sending me a text.

Celine: *OMG – there's been a bomb threat and they've canceled the after-party!!!*

Me: *You're kidding?! Where are you?*

Celine: *Getting ready to leave. Where are you? Do you need a ride home?*

Me: *I'm at Mason's hotel. He's taking a shower and doesn't know about it yet.*

Celine sent me an emoji with its tongue hanging out.

I chuckled and sent her one back with a smiley face.

Celine: *Why aren't you in there washing his back?*

Me: *Very funny.*

Celine: *Seriously though. Do you need a ride?*

I didn't want to disappear while he was in the shower, and yet, if we weren't going to the after-party, there was no reason to stick around.

Before I could figure out what to tell her, Mason walked out of the bedroom, holding his phone and wearing nothing but a towel slung low around his waist. Those two hipbone lines that made girls stupid tapered down and disappeared behind the towel. I forced my eyes to stay on his as he spoke. "I just found out they canceled the after-party because of a bomb threat."

I held up my phone. "Celine just texted me about it, too."

"Aside from the bomb-threat, I'm kind of relieved. I'm not much of a party-animal," he admitted. "I do it for the publicity, but I'd much rather just stay here and kick back."

He seemed really casual about the bomb-threat. "Has this ever happened to you before?"

"The bomb threat? Yeah. I'm pretty sure it's Stalker John,"

he said, and told me about him.

"You're kidding?" I replied. "So, he's been threatening your life? Do you think it's serious?"

"Honestly, I don't know. Someone tried breaking into my house recently," he replied. "We think that was him, too."

"Wow."

He sighed. "He's another reason we've tried to keep the after-parties private. The location must have somehow leaked out. If you noticed, the address wasn't on the pass. Just a phone number with a recording."

"I saw that."

"I wish they'd find and arrest him before he actually harms someone."

"But, you think he's the culprit?"

"I can't say for sure, but probably. None of it started happening until he showed up in my life. Being famous has made me a lot of enemies, but this guy takes the cake."

My phone chimed again.

"It's Celine asking if I need a ride. I should get going," I told him.

"Wait. I don't know about you, but I'm starving. Join me for room service? Afterward, I'll have my driver bring you home."

I bit my lower lip.

"Nothing else, if that's what you're thinking. I'll be good," he replied, smiling.

Screw it. I was already there, and the mention of food was making my stomach growl again.

"Okay."

He grinned. "Good. I'll hurry up and we'll order something. The menu is on the desk over there. Take a look at it while I shower."

"Sure."

He left me alone again and I sent Celine a text, explaining what we were doing.

Celine: *Sounds romantic. Make sure he uses protection.*

Me: *Nothing is going to happen! We already discussed it.*

Celine: *For real?*

Me: *Yes. I'll tell you all about it the next time we talk.*

Celine: *You'd better. Night.*

Me: *Night.*

I shoved my phone into my purse and got up to grab the menu he'd told me about. As I looked through it, I could feel my eyelids getting tired. Yawning, I set it down, deciding on a chicken Caesar salad, although what I really wanted was a burger and fries. I stretched out on the sofa and within seconds, drifted off to sleep.

Chapter 15

Mason

After my shower, I found Terra asleep on the sofa. I thought about waking her up, but she looked so peaceful I decided to let her rest. Plus, I had a feeling that as soon as she ate, she'd want to leave. I wasn't ready to let her go just yet.

Although the sofa looked pretty comfortable, I thought about carrying her to my bed, but knew she might get the wrong idea. Instead, I grabbed a blanket, covered her up, and dimmed the lights.

As much as I wanted to sleep, I was too restless. After lying in bed for an hour, tossing and turning, I turned on the television and began channel surfing. It must have been too loud because Terra was suddenly standing in the doorway.

"Oh, shit. I'm sorry," I said, sitting up. "I woke you."

She smiled. "You should have done it earlier. Sorry I fell asleep."

"No apologies. You were obviously exhausted."

She walked in and sat down on the chair across from the bed. "I should get going."

"Why don't you just stay the rest of the night and we'll get breakfast later? Or, we could grab something to eat right now. Like we were planning on in the first place."

Terra yawned. "I don't know if I'll be able to stay awake long enough to eat."

I shoved the covers off me and noticed with amusement

how she was relieved to see I had on pair of boxers. "Here… you take the bed and I'll go lie down on the sofa."

Her eyes widened. "No. I couldn't take your bed. I'll just grab a taxi and go home."

"It's late. Please. Stay," I said softly.

She let out a sigh and then smiled. "Fine, but I'm not letting you give up your bed for me."

I waved my hand toward the mattress. "It's king-sized. There's room for both of us. Don't worry, I won't lay a finger on you."

Terra chuckled. "Again, I don't know if I should be relieved or offended. Anyway, I thought you were the one worried I'd try and attack you?"

"I still am… so you're going to have to try and control yourself."

Gasping, she grabbed a pillow and hit me with it. Laughing, I grabbed one of the others and hit her back. It quickly turned into an all-out pillow fight, and the woman didn't take any prisoners…

Terra

I was much better at pillow-fighting than Mason, but I had a feeling he was going easy on me. After I wailed on him a few more times, he snatched the pillow out of my hands, picked me up over his shoulder, and dropped me onto the bed. Shocked that he was strong enough to handle me like he was, all I could do was stare up at him.

"Here," he said, tossing me one of the pillows.

"So, I'm staying for sure?" I asked, putting it under my head.

"Yes." He lay down next to me. Folding his hands under his head, he smiled. "See, this isn't so bad, is it?"

"It's actually a nice mattress," I replied, running my hand over the fabric. "What is it, one of those expensive air beds?"

"Yeah." He grabbed one of the remote controls sitting on the nightstand and handed it to me. "Here, you may as well find your sleep number."

I played around with the buttons until I found a comfortable level of air, and then relaxed while Mason settled back into bed.

"Do you mind if I watch TV?" he asked.

"No. It's fine." My eyelids were getting heavy again and the bed was so comfortable, it wouldn't take much to fall asleep. "Did you ever find out anything more about the bomb threat?"

"No. Someone called it in from an anonymous number."

"Do you think it was just a prank?"

"Maybe. The problem is that they knew where the after-party was being held. Either someone who received an invite made the bomb threat, or one of our staff opened their mouths."

"Or one of the people throwing the party for you guys."

"Yeah."

"That sucks."

He nodded.

I yawned. "Hopefully they'll figure it out."

"Hopefully."

I closed my eyes. "Goodnight."

"Goodnight," he said softly.

I SLEPT DEEPLY. When I did finally wake up, a sliver of light peeked through the heavy curtains, making the room more visible. I'd almost forgotten where I was until I noticed the dark head next to mine.

Mason.

He was still sleeping, which gave me time to study his face, which was boyishly handsome at that moment. It was hard to believe I was lying next to one of the most famous men in America, one who was down-to-earth and not at all what I'd expected. The tabloids made him out to be a bad boy who loved partying and women. Talking to him last night, however, I learned he was much more than that. Yeah, he'd tested me, which was kind of bullshit, but thinking about it, I couldn't exactly blame him. And, if he really was just after sex, he could have dropped me off and gotten some from any number of different women. Maybe it was all an act, but after having slept in the same bed with him all night, I had no reason to doubt him. Of course, I wasn't supermodel material. But, he had told me that he found me sexy. He didn't have to tell me that.

Mason's eyes opened.

Embarrassed to be caught staring at him, I quickly looked away, sat up, and stretched my arms.

"Sleep well?" he asked, rubbing his eye.

"Yes. Better than I have in long time. I should get one of these beds," I replied. "I wonder how much they cost?"

"I've seen them upwards of ten-thousand dollars," he replied.

My eyes widened. "For a bed? That's insane."

He grinned. "I won't tell you how much my bed at home was if you think that's crazy."

Now I wanted to know. "What? More than that?"

"A little," he replied, although from the light in his eyes, it was probably much more.

It wasn't any of my business, so I decided to change the subject. I wasn't exactly broke, but we were worlds apart financially.

"Would you mind if I took a shower?" I asked.

"No. Be my guest. But let me use the bathroom first."

"Of course." I scooted to the edge of the bed and stood up. Looking down, I saw that my poor dress was horribly wrinkled.

"Crap. I wish I had something else to wear," I said, sighing. "All I have is the concert T-shirt I purchased last night and this thing."

"Don't worry about it. You look fine," he replied, standing up.

My eyes almost popped out of my head when he turned and I noticed the flagpole in his boxers. I'd forgotten about morning hard-ons. I quickly averted my gaze and began picking lint off the dress. "I'll, um, figure something out."

"If you want, you can wear your T-shirt and a pair of my sweats," he replied, walking over to his suitcase. He pulled out a pair of gray ones and held them out. "Here. These are clean."

"I doubt they'd fit me," I replied, thinking of his slender hips compared to mine.

"Just try them and if they don't, you can wear the dress."

"Okay. Thanks." Trying not to stare at the tent in his shorts, I took the sweats.

He shut the suitcase and then headed toward the bathroom, his boner bobbing up and down. "By the way, if you want I can have breakfast sent up here. Or we can eat out. Either way, I'm fine with whatever you decide."

"You should pick."

He was quiet for a few seconds and then his face lit up. "We're going out. There's this place in Moundsview I used to go to all the time. They serve pancakes as big as your plate and eight-egg omelets that are kick ass."

"RJ's?" I asked, remembering the little hole-in-the-wall. He was right, though. They had excellent food.

"That's it! I haven't been there in years. Is it still open?"

I nodded.

"Sweet. Let's go there. We'll sneak out and catch a cab."

"Sneak out?"

"Yeah. I want a normal breakfast without having everyone staring at us in the restaurant. Especially if we pull up in a limo and walk in with security."

"Uh, okay. How are we going to sneak out?"

He grinned. "I have my ways."

Chapter 16

Mason

I had to admire Terra. She had class and didn't even comment on my morning erection, which I'd pretended to ignore.

After using the bathroom, she went in and took her shower. As I waited, my cell phone rang. It was Zed.

"Hey, what's up?" I asked him.

"I was wondering if you wanted to catch breakfast."

"I can't. I have stuff to do."

"Bummer. Okay, maybe we can catch dinner?"

We usually did our own thing so I wondered what was up. "I might be busy all day." *With Terra, I hoped.*

He laughed. "Does it have something to do with that chick with the big hooters?"

"No," I lied. It was none of his business.

"Oh. Did you two hook up last night?"

"Nope."

"Damn, I would have been all over that."

"We're just friends."

"That's cool. You don't have her number, do you? Since we're not leaving for a couple days, I wouldn't mind getting to know her."

In other words, he wanted to fuck her. "I don't have it."

"But you're friends?" he asked, not believing me.

"More like acquaintances."

"You have her name?"

"Terra."

"Terra what?"

"Just Terra. I don't know her last name."

"Or how to get ahold of her?"

"Right."

"Why do I feel like you're trying to keep her for yourself?" he asked, sounding amused.

"Why would I do that?" I asked. "She's not my type."

Terra

I was drying myself off when I heard Mason on the phone. My name was mentioned, so I knew they were talking about me. I pressed my ear to the door to listen.

"Why would I do that? She's *not* my type."

The scorn in his voice as he said it felt like a punch in the gut. So that was why he hadn't touched me. I wasn't his 'type'. As much as it shouldn't have bothered me, it did.

"I'll probably never talk to her again," he said, still on the phone. More words were said and it sounded like he didn't want to have anything more to do with me.

Fine, I thought angrily.

If I wasn't good enough for him, I certainly wasn't going to waste my morning having breakfast with Mr. Super Star.

I quickly got dressed, ignoring the sweats and the T-shirt and put my dress back on. I ran my fingers through my hair and then stepped out of the bathroom.

"Didn't they fit?" Mason asked, now off the phone.

"What?" I snapped.

His eyes widened. "The sweats?"

"I don't know. I have to go," I replied, walking to the door to put my shoes on.

"What do you mean you have to go? I thought we were having breakfast together?" he asked, looking confused.

"I changed my mind." My pride wouldn't let me explain what I'd heard. Chances were he'd lie about the conversation to make me feel better. "I have a lot of stuff to do today."

"Oh."

After slipping on my heels, I opened the door.

"Wait, I'll take you home."

I turned and looked at him. "I already called an Uber," I lied.

"Cancel it"

"I'd rather not."

He walked over and stared down at me. "What's wrong?"

"Why does there have to be something wrong?"

"Because I can tell you're angry."

"I'm fine," I said, looking away. "I have to go."

"Terra—"

Ignoring him, I walked out of his room and passed by a

couple security guards having a conversation in the hallway. They stopped talking and gaped at me. I figured they were shocked to find a woman like me leaving Mason Stone's hotel room. A woman who was obviously not... his 'type'.

Chapter 17

Mason

I didn't understand why Terra was pissed, but it was obvious she was. And it had something to do with me.

Grabbing my jeans, I quickly slipped them on and left my suite, determined to find out what went wrong. Unfortunately, by the time I made it down to the main lobby, I couldn't find her. Making matters worse, my security guards started asking me questions, wanting to help but only frustrating me further.

"Just don't worry about it," I grumbled, heading back to the elevators.

Once I was back in my room, I found Terra's business card and tried calling her. She didn't pick up, so I left her a message asking her to call me. Something told me she wouldn't, but I wasn't ready to give up.

AN HOUR LATER, after showering and changing into jeans and a hoodie, I slipped down to the room below mine and snuck out. I took the staircase and almost ran into Mack, who was standing in the lobby, staring down at his cell phone. Pulling my hood up, I kept my head down, stepped out of the building, and headed to Terra's bakery. When I arrived, I noticed Cindy was working again.

"Oh, you're back," she said, staring at me happily.

"Yeah. Is Terra around?"

Her smile fell. "No. She took today off."

"So, she didn't stop by this morning?"

"No."

An older woman walked out of the back room carrying a tray of cookies. Noticing me, she smiled and said hello.

"Hello," I replied back.

"Is there something we can help you with?" she asked.

Thinking that she looked a lot like Terra, I wondered if the woman was her mother. I looked at the tag on her shirt. Her name was Marcella.

"I was looking for Terra."

"She's off today," the woman said, looking intrigued.

"I heard. You wouldn't happen to have her address?" I asked.

"Dammit to hell, I... I can't give it to you," Marcella said. "Motherfucker."

My eyes widened at the harsh language. Had Terra already told her about me? "Okay. When will she be in next?"

"What's this about?" Marcella asked, her eyes narrowing.

"He wants to order a birthday cake," Cindy said.

Marcella relaxed. "We can help you with that."

"I'd prefer to talk to Terra, if I may?"

"She'll be in tomorrow morning. I'll let her know you stopped by," Cindy said. "What was your name? I don't think I ever caught it."

"Thanks. I'll check back tomorrow," I replied, not answering her. Shoving my hands into my pockets, I turned and walked out the door.

Terra

When I left the hotel, I thought about going to Sweet Treats, but knew Marcella was in and I wasn't in the mood for explanations. She'd take one look at me and know that something was wrong, especially since I was wearing a fancy, wrinkled dress on a Sunday morning. Instead, I walked down the street to a coffee shop, ordered an iced latte, and then ordered an Uber. As I waited, Mason called and left me a message. Ignoring it, I shoved my phone back into my purse and told myself to forget about him. He was obviously an asshole. A strange one, but still an asshole.

The car dropped me off in front of my building and just when I thought the day couldn't get any worse, I ran into Anna and Sonny as the car pulled away.

"Hello," Sonny said, looking uncomfortable.

I nodded but didn't reply.

"Wow, late night?" Anna asked, noticing I still had my clothing on from yesterday.

"Yep." Holding my head up high, I walked past them.

"Where'd you go?" Sonny asked.

Without thinking, I told them.

"So, you were there? Wasn't his concert incredible?" said Anna.

I turned and looked back at her. "It was okay. I'm not really a fan of his music."

"Mason Stone's?" she said, her eyes widening. "I think he's amazing."

"He thinks he's pretty wonderful too," I replied.

"Rock stars usually do," Sonny replied.

"He definitely does." I grinned coolly. "We hung out last night. He's kind of a dick."

Anna gasped. "You're kidding? You met him?"

Enjoying the look of envy in her eyes, I nodded. "We actually spent the night together."

Sonny snorted. "Right."

"Believe what you want. I don't care," I replied, turning back around.

"Wait a second," Anna said, walking over to me. "Did you really get together with him?"

"Yeah. Here," I said, pulling out my phone. I showed her a couple of the pictures Celine had taken and sent to me. Some were of the pre-party, when we'd walked through the crowd, and the last was after the concert, when we were backstage.

"Oh, my God, you *did* meet him," she said, staring at my phone in awe. "Was he the one who picked you in the limo yesterday?"

"Yeah," I lied.

"Let me see the pictures," Sonny mumbled.

I held my phone up, showing him the one where Mason had his arm around my shoulders. He stared at it for a few seconds and then looked at me. "How in the world did you two meet? You never once mentioned anything about knowing this guy when we were together."

"That's because I met him after. At the bakery last week, in fact," I replied.

"And he asked you out?" Sonny replied, still looking skeptical.

"There's more to it than that, but… we did spend the night together, which is why I'm still in my dress."

"And he made you Uber home?" she asked, looking at me with pity.

"No. We were supposed to go to breakfast, but I was too tired from all of the sex we had. The guy was an animal," I replied with a straight face. "And I knew he'd probably want more afterward, so I snuck out. I can barely walk as it is."

Anna and Sonny both stared at me in shock.

Feeling a little better about the morning, I turned and headed into the building, my head held high as I did the *walk of shame*.

Twenty minutes later, I was sitting in front of my television with a bowl of spumoni ice cream and a Diet Coke, depressed and feeling like crap. As I flipped through the channels, my phone buzzed again. It was Celine.

Celine: *Hey, how's everything going??*

Me: *Fine. I'm at home now.*

Celine: *I want details.*

Me: *There are none.*

Celine: *Don't make me come over there.*

I sighed. She would, too.

Me: *Nothing happened. We fell asleep and I took an Uber home.*

Celine: *For real?*

Me: *Yeah.*

Celine: *He didn't try anything?*

Me: *Nope. I'm apparently not his type.*

Celine: *He told you that?*

Me: *No, but I heard him tell someone else.*

Celine: *What a fucking asshole. You're too good for him.*

I sent her a smiley face.

Celine: *You want to grab lunch?*

Me: *I'm eating now.*

Celine: *Dinner later?*

Me: *Not tonight. I'm tired and just want to rest.*

Celine: *You okay?*

Me: *Of course. Just because I'm not Mason Stone's type doesn't mean that my life is over.*

Celine: *You got that right. Forget about him. I'm throwing out all of his CDs and erasing his songs from my iPod.*

Smiling, I told her she didn't have to.

Celine: *I know but I have to now that I know what kind of prick he is.*

I sent her a heart.

Celine: *Love you, girl. Let's get together this week.*

Me: *Okay. Love you, too.*

We texted a few more words to each other and then I put my phone away. As I was about to take another bite of my ice cream, someone called my home phone. It was my aunt Marcella. She never usually called so I was immediately worried.

"Is everything okay?" I asked.

"Terra?" Marcella replied.

"Sorry. Yes, it's me. What's up?"

"A man stopped in asking for you a few minutes ago. He wouldn't give us his name, but Cindy said he was in the other day and wanted to order a cake."

"Uh, okay. What did he want?"

"He wanted your address."

My eyes widened. "You didn't give it to him, did you?" I asked, panicking. With my luck, Mason could be on his way over right now.

"No. Of course not, dammit to hell. I would never give a stranger your address."

I relaxed.

"At any rate, we told him you'd be in tomorrow. He's going to probably stop in."

Crap.

"Okay. Thanks, Marcella."

"He was very handsome."

"Yeah." Although, I had to admit he'd become less attractive now that I knew what a jerk he really was.

"He wouldn't let us help him. He just wanted to talk to you."

"I'll take care of him tomorrow."

"Okay. Oh, are you going to be at your mom's tonight?"

I'd forgotten all about the lasagna dinner and Tyler. There was no way in hell I wanted to deal with that after everything else. I wasn't in the mood.

"No. I'm too tired."

"You should go. I think she has some big announcement she plans on making."

Now *that* surprised me. "What big announcement?"

"If I knew, I'd tell you. Whatever it is, I think it's important, though. She practically begged me to come tonight. You should try and make it, too."

Groaning inwardly, I told her I'd try.

"Good. I have to go. We're getting busy."

"Okay. See you later."

"Hopefully tonight."

We hung up and I thought about my mom. I really didn't want to go anywhere, but I was intrigued with whatever it was she wanted to tell everyone. I decided to call her. As I was about to do just that, my phone started ringing again. Recognizing Mason's number, I decided to answer it. I didn't want to keep playing games and I certainly didn't want him showing up and making some kind of scene at the bakery.

"Hello," I murmured.

"Terra? It's Mason."

"Yeah. Hi."

"What's going on?"

"Nothing. I'm kind of busy though and can't really talk."

"Are you mad at me?" he replied.

"No," I lied.

"Then why are you ignoring me and why did you leave so abruptly?"

I took a deep breath. "Let me ask *you* a question. The same one from last night—what in the hell do you want from me?"

"I thought I told you—I want to get to know you better. I like you. A lot."

"So, you want to be friends?" I said a little dryly.

"Yeah. Maybe more."

"I thought I wasn't your type."

"My type? What are you... wait a second. Were you listening in on my conversation earlier this morning?"

"I wasn't listening in. Not on purpose, at least. You were loud enough that I heard you in the bathroom."

"Okay," he said, sounding amused. "Now everything is starting to make sense. I thought maybe I'd done something to really piss you off."

"I have to go," I replied, getting upset again. Could he not see that his words were hurtful?

"Wait. When I told Zed that you weren't my type, I only did that because I didn't want him to know we were going to be hanging out."

"So, you're embarrassed to be seen around me?"

"*What?* No. Not at all. I just don't want them to know about you. Otherwise they'd be into my business and my private life isn't something I like sharing. Even with them."

"Listen, if I wasn't into you, would I be calling and texting you all morning?"

He had a point.

"Terra, I want to get to know you. I'm not lying and I don't know any other way to convince you of that."

He sounded sincere. Maybe I'd overreacted.

"Look, I'm sorry you heard the conversation. I can imagine how I would have felt if the tables were turned. I swear to you, though, you *are* my type. You're beautiful, intelligent, and sexy as all hell."

I smiled.

"If you want to know the truth, I barely slept last night just thinking about all of the things I wanted to do to you," he replied softly. "It was hard keeping my hands to myself."

My stomach turned to molten lava. "Really?"

"Yeah. I don't know if you noticed, but this morning I was pretty riled up."

"Riled up?" I asked, knowing what he meant, but wanting to hear him say it.

"Excited. Hard."

I chuckled. "I may have noticed. I attributed it to having to pee."

He chuckled. "I needed to do more than that, but like I said before, I don't want our relationship to be based on sex."

My stomach filled with butterflies. *Relationship?*

"So, what are you doing right now?"

I stared at my ice cream bowl and it suddenly didn't look appetizing at all. "Just sitting here at home."

"Let's get together."

"Okay. When?"

"How about right now?"

I bit my lip in contemplation. Did I want him to know where I lived? Deciding I didn't care either way, I replied, "I guess so. Would you like my address?"

"I already have it."

This surprised me. My phone number wasn't in any address book. It was unlisted. "How?"

"I'm rich and money talks."

I snorted. "So you paid someone for my address?"

"Pretty much. I know people who know how to find things."

"Apparently. So, what's my address?"

He told me.

"Yeah. That's it. How long will it take you to get here?"

"Hold on a minute, okay?"

"Sure." Holding the phone to my ear, I picked up the bowl of ice cream and headed to the kitchen. As I set it on the counter, my doorbell rang.

He chuckled into the phone. "Honey… I'm home…"

Chapter 18

Mason

When Terra answered the door, her face was flushed and her expression was almost comical. I'd obviously shocked the hell out of her.

I smiled. "Hi."

She shook her head and smiled back. "What would you have done if I'd have said 'no'?"

"Camped out here in the hallway until you changed your mind."

She laughed. "You're crazy."

"Yes, I am. Among other things. Can I come in?"

"Sure." She moved aside and I stepped into her condo. It was small, but nicely decorated in what I recognized as being a Shabby Chic style — very feminine and white, with a lot of vintage-looking furniture and tossed pillows everywhere.

"Make yourself at home," she said, looking a little anxious.

I sat down on the sofa and stared up at her. She'd changed into a pair of yoga pants and a gray T-shirt.

"So, I take it someone let you through the security doors?"

"Yeah. These two teenaged girls. They thought I looked like Mason Stone, which is the only reason, I'm sure, they let me in," I replied, thinking back in amusement at their expressions when they first saw me.

121

"You didn't acknowledge that you were?"

"Oh, hell no. They'd post about it on social media and this place would turn into a circus. Plus, Mack doesn't know I'm gone."

"Snuck out again, huh?" I asked, chuckling.

"Yeah. Nice place, by the way," I said, looking around. She really did have a flair for decorating, although it wasn't exactly my style. It was much too girly.

Terra glanced around. "Thanks."

My cell phone began to buzz. I took it out of my pocket and saw that it was Zed, asking if I wanted to hang out. "You hungry? I never did get breakfast," I told Terra as I sent him a message about being busy.

"A little. How did you get here?"

I looked up at her. "I called a cab. You have a car, right?"

"Yeah."

"Then let's go to RJ's."

"Okay. Let me change first," she said, backing away.

"You look fine," I replied. "RJ's isn't anything fancy."

"I know, but this has a hole in it," she said, raising the corner of her T-shirt. "And these yoga pants aren't doing me any favors."

My eyes lowered to her curvy thighs. I thought she looked fine but didn't want to argue. "Whatever you want to do."

"It'll just take me a couple of minutes. I'll be right back. The remote control is on the coffee table, if you want to watch TV while I'm changing."

I nodded my thanks, and sat back on the sofa. I watched

122

with appreciation as her thick, biteable ass swished away in those sexy-as-fuck yoga pants and wished she would just keep them on.

I adjusted myself through my jeans, and picked up a magazine that was lying on her side table.

Terra

I quickly changed into a newer pair of shiny black leggings and a light brown V-neck sweater. Afterward, I raced into the bathroom, pulled my hair back into a loose French braid, applied some makeup, and added a spritz of perfume. Resolved that it was the best I could do in such a short time, I went back to the living room, where I found Mason looking through one of my fashion magazines.

"Having fun?" I asked, amused.

"I'm reading this very educational article directed at women. It's explains how to please a man in bed."

"Oh? Is it accurate?" I asked, as if I hadn't read the entire article more than once. After losing Sonny to the slut down the hallway, I'd wondered if there'd been something I could have done different sexually. According to the article, men liked women willing to experiment. Admittedly, I hadn't been very adventurous or spontaneous. But neither had he.

Mason tapped on the page he was reading. "All of the things it mentions will definitely work, but... the truth is, a woman just needs to be naked and willing to have sex. We're pretty simple creatures."

"Does that go for any woman?"

"If he desires her, yeah. Pretty much. She just needs to be ready, able, and interested." He waggled his eyebrows.

I chuckled. "If my memory serves me right, it seems like you're more interested in the ones *not* interested."

"Correction. I'm not interested in gold-diggers or groupies who put out just because I'm a celebrity."

"Can I just say that you're not exactly a homely looking guy, so I doubt that's the only reason women want you."

"So, you're saying I'm not ugly?"

Even with his messy hair and five-o'clock shadow, which was making an early appearance, he was a heartbreaker. "No."

He looked back down at the magazine, smiling. "Back to this article. After our little discussion, I wish this talked about pleasing women instead. Each one is different and it can be intimidating trying to figure out what works and what doesn't."

"Are you saying you have difficulties in that area?" I teased, feeling more comfortable with him. I liked his sarcasm and dry humor.

"I haven't had any complaints. But, I'm also a perfectionist. I'll do whatever it takes to make sure a woman leaves my bed breathless and smiling. Of course, it's been a while since I've had sex, so I'm probably rusty. Hell, the next woman might even leave my bed gasping in laughter."

That was interesting. I wondered how long 'a while' was. For a gorgeous guy like him, I imagined we were looking at, like, two weeks, tops.

I snorted. "Isn't it supposed to be like riding a bike? Once you learn, you never forget?"

"Right, but you can still fall off and get injured. End up with hospital bills and a permanent limp."

I laughed.

He set the magazine down. "We should go. All of this talk about sex isn't helping our cause."

"Which is?"

"Abstinence."

"Right."

"Neither is that sweater. Let's get out of here."

Mason insisted on driving, explaining that he didn't get the chance to very often and missed being behind the wheel. I gladly handed him my keys and we headed to the underground garage, where my Enclave was parked.

"By the way, you look and smell very nice," he said, starting the engine. "Again."

I grinned. "Thanks."

He stared at me for a few seconds and I almost thought he was going to kiss me, but then his cell phone went off. Sighing, he checked it and scowled.

"What's wrong?"

"It's Mack. He's insisting I call him." He put his phone down.

"You're not going to?"

"I'll do it later. If it was that important he'd send me a text explaining things. He just wants me to check in."

"What is he, your father?"

"Exactly. I never get any privacy or peace. Don't get me wrong; I'm grateful for everything I have, but lately, I've been missing my old life."

"Your life before you became famous?"

He nodded. "Yeah. It was fun for a while, but now it's just becoming a headache. I guess it wouldn't be so bad if I was given more space. I shouldn't have to sneak out to enjoy a day like today with a beautiful woman."

Flattered, I smiled. "It's for your own protection, though, right? Because of that stalker you have?"

"Yeah, but I'm not afraid of him. I'd actually like to meet the asshole face-to-face and deal with it that way."

"If he's psychotic, which it sounds like he is, that might be a horrible idea."

"Maybe… maybe not. I just want to get rid of the guy and move on."

I nodded.

"Anyway, enough about me. Tell me about yourself. Where did you grow up?"

We spent the rest of the drive talking about my family and how I became interested in opening my own bakery. He told me how impressed he'd been seeing the picture of the castle cake I'd made.

"So, you experienced a little of the limelight during that show, I imagine," he said, talking about my 15 minutes of fame on *Cake Queens*.

"Yeah, but nothing like what you're used to. They did put us up in a hotel for the weekend, in Hollywood, and paid for everything. So that was nice."

"What were the judges like?"

"Very critical on camera, but nice and polite when the camera wasn't rolling," I replied, thinking back. There'd been four judges, all celebrities in their own rights. Three of them had their own cooking shows and the fourth helped failing restaurants reinvent themselves in a wildly popular series that still ran. "Did you ever watch the show?"

"No. To be honest I don't watch a lot of TV. I'd rather spend the time working on songs."

"Speaking of which, I thought you were going to play some of your music for me." I looked at him, challenge in my gaze.

He flicked his eyes to me and then put his attention back on the road as he smiled. "You're going to hold me to it, huh?"

"Of course."

"How about tonight?"

I suddenly remembered my mother's dinner party. Although I would have loved hanging out with him, something told me I needed to be there. An idea came to me, but I didn't think he'd go for it.

"I actually have plans, but… if you want to join me, we can go back to your hotel afterward and you can play me something."

"Actually, I would love to join you," he replied, smiling.

I smirked. "You don't even know what it is yet."

"I'm game for anything that includes you."

"Even if it includes dinner at my mom's?"

He gave me a sour look. "That might not be a good idea. I

think I may have met her at the bakery today. She called me a motherfucker. That's probably a good indicator that she wouldn't want me at her dinner table."

"My mother? Oh, that would have been my aunt. Don't take it personal. She calls everyone a motherfucker."

"Tough crowd, your family," he said wryly.

I explained about the Tourette's syndrome.

"She'll be there, too. Just ignore it when she swears. I can tell it embarrasses her. It's better to just not acknowledge it."

"I could curse, too. You know, make her feel like less of an outsider?" he asked with a smile.

I snorted. "No. Absolutely not. My mother would kick you out of the house so quickly, you wouldn't know what hit you."

"And I probably wouldn't get dinner, right?" he added.

"Exactly. And she's a fabulous cook."

"What about dessert?"

"I'm pretty sure you wouldn't get that, either."

"What if I lick my plate? I've been told I'm pretty skilled in that area," he said with a wicked smile.

My girly parts fluttered, and I resisted the urge to squirm in my seat.

He gave me an innocent look. "Get your mind out of the gutter, lady. I'm talking about food. Nothing more."

Right...

Chapter 19

Mason

I was having a really good time with Terra. She was fun to talk to and just as much of a smartass as I was, if not more. By the time we arrived at RJ's, I learned a lot about her family and friends, especially Celine, who she'd been friends with for many years.

"What about you? Are your parents still living in Minnesota?" she asked after the waitress took our order.

"My mother died when I was a kid. As far as my old man, I don't know where he is. I wish I did." I told her about his drinking problem and how, after my mother had died, he'd had a nervous breakdown. "He's basically disappeared off the face of the earth. I've tried finding him, even hired a private investigator, but nobody has been able to locate him. I have to wonder if he's even still alive."

"That's too bad. I'm sorry to hear that," she replied softly.

I nodded.

"You don't have any other family?"

"No. Just my bandmates and Mack."

"Are you close to them?" she asked, curiosity dancing in her beautiful green eyes.

I got lost in them for a minute before I pulled myself back to the conversation. "Not really. I mean, we're good friends, but probably nothing like you and Celine. It sounds like you two are more like sisters."

"We are. I don't know what I'd do without her."

"It's good to have close friends. To be honest, I've always been kind of a loner. Don't get me wrong, I enjoy hanging out with the guys and stuff, but I also need my space."

"Space is a good thing. I need mine, too. I think it's why I love designing cakes. I can spend hours decorating and prefer to be alone while I'm doing it. It's relaxing."

"You're a true artist. I'd love to see more of your cake designs."

"I have some photo albums at home I could show you. Speaking of which, do you still need a birthday cake?"

"Yeah. My birthday isn't for another month, but I'd really love for you to make it."

"What kind of theme are you thinking?"

"I'm not sure yet," I told her honestly.

"What are you into?"

I chuckled. "Music. Obviously."

"I could work with that." She threw me a smile. "Anything else?"

"Right now, just you," I said softly.

Her cheeks turned pink and she smiled.

"Have you ever jumped out of a cake before?" I asked, imagining her nearly naked in heels, white pasties, and a thong. The thought of licking frosting off her body was enough to get me sprung again.

I really need to get laid.

Terra laughed. "No. Never."

"Would you?"

She shrugged. "I guess it depends on who the cake was

for."

"Me."

Terra looked at me like I was on drugs, and then shook her head. "I don't know. Maybe?"

"Maybe? I guess that's better than a 'no'."

"If I were to ever pop out of a cake, it wouldn't be cheap, you know."

"I have some money saved," I quipped, smiling.

"You're crazy, you know that?"

I winked. "*Now* you're getting to know the real me."

"Yes, and it's a little scary."

I lifted an eyebrow, trying not to laugh. "You still want to introduce me to your mother?"

"Are you kidding, she's going to love you. And not because you're famous. In fact, I've been thinking. I don't think we shouldn't tell her who you really are."

"Whatever you want to do," I replied, feeling relieved.

"I just don't want her to be judgmental. She wouldn't want her daughter being corrupted by a bad boy rock star, no matter how famous you are."

I wiggled my eyebrows. "I am kind of a bad boy, aren't I?"

"To be honest, you're one of the nicest guys I've met in a very long time."

Something weird and warm swirled in my belly at her sincerity. "Thank you. Just keep it to yourself, though." I paused and looked around the tiny restaurant where people of all ages happily chatted and ate their meals without even giving me a second glance. "It's bad for my image. That's what my publicist says, at least."

"I won't say a word." She bit back a smile.

The waitress stopped at the table with our food.

"Just like I remembered," I replied, as the woman set down two plates in front of me—one with eggs, bacon, sausage, hash browns, and toast. The other had a stack of blueberry pancakes that were as wide as the plate itself.

"Wow. This omelet is huge," Terra said, staring down at her own dish with amusement. She'd ordered the Ranchero Omelet and it was covered with cheese and some kind of green chili sauce. The waitress had recommended it.

"That one only has six eggs. You should see the big one," the woman said, setting a bottle of ketchup down on the table. "It has ten."

"Yowza," she replied.

"Say, you look familiar," the waitress said, staring down at me.

"I used to come here back when I was a teenager. My old man used to bring me."

"I've worked here for years so I may have served you before. You from around here?"

"No," I replied. "But, we loved driving out here every Saturday morning for breakfast."

"Used to, huh? Your old man still eat here?"

"I don't think so," I replied, frowning, my heart heavy.

"What's his name?" she asked.

"Len Stone."

Her eyes widened. "Len?"

I nodded.

"Oh, my God, Len *Stone*?" she said, looking excited. "That means you're Mason, right?"

Shit. My stomach took a dive. I didn't want to be recognized. "Uh, yeah."

She clucked her tongue and gave me a wistful look. "Your old man used to talk about you all the time. He was so proud of you. Still is, I'm sure."

"Thanks," I replied, feeling uncomfortable. Something told me the meal was going to turn into a media fiasco.

As if reading my mind, she lowered her voice. "Hey, don't worry being here, Mason. I won't tell anyone who you really are. Len used to say that you were shy about being a celebrity. That you hated the limelight and people pestering you."

I wondered how he'd known, considering we hadn't spoken in years.

"Thanks," I replied, grateful.

She patted my shoulder. "Don't you worry about a thing." She pointed at herself. "Sally takes care of her customers, even the famous ones. All I ask is for an autograph before you leave. Maybe two — one for the credit card receipt, and one for me." She winked. "Unless you're paying in cash. In that case, I'll still want an autograph."

I chuckled. "Definitely."

"Let me know if there's anything else you need," Sally said.

"Will do. You, uh, haven't seen my old man in here lately, have you?" I asked.

"No. Not for a couple of weeks. He doesn't say much to

anyone when he comes in, either. Of course, he's usually with the woman I was talking about. Is she your stepmom?"

Chapter 20

Terra

I could tell from the look on Mason's face that he was totally blown out of the water by what she'd said.

"I... don't know," he replied, his eyes wide. "You said he was here a couple of weeks ago?"

"Yeah. Two Saturdays ago, if I recall." The waitress's forehead scrunched up as she studied his face. "Pardon me for asking, but are you two not talking?"

He sat back against the booth. "Something like that. How often does he come in these days?"

"Maybe twice a month. Like I said, he's usually with this friendly-looking woman and they keep to themselves. They hold hands sometimes and smile a lot. I'd say they were in love," Sally replied with a little smile.

"You're sure it's my dad? Len?" he asked.

Sally nodded. "Yeah. Same guy who used to bring you in here, only he—don't take this the wrong way—seems like he's in a better place."

"My dad has a drinking problem," Mason admitted. "It's one of the reasons we drifted apart."

She smiled sadly. "That's too bad. You know, I figured he might have had some problems. He always looked hungover or smelled like booze when he used to stop in, even after you weren't in the picture. But, that was a while ago. Now his eyes are clear and he looks... content. Especially with the woman he's with."

Mason's eyes grew misty. He quickly looked down at his food and began buttering his pancakes. "Well, I'm glad he finally found someone to make him happy."

My heart went out to him. I had a feeling this news was bittersweet. He wanted his father to be happy, but even more so, wanted to be part of the reason.

"You want me to call you the next time he comes in?" she asked. "I could do that. I work every Saturday."

"Yeah, that would be great. Or, maybe you could give him my number?" he replied.

"I'll do both. How about that?" Sally replied, pulling out a pen. "What's your number?"

He gave it to her. "Just don't give it to anyone else."

"Don't you worry about a thing," she said, folding the piece of paper and slipping it into her bra. "It's our little secret… and in a safe spot. Too safe, if you ask me."

We both laughed.

She smiled. "Listen, kids, I'll let you get on with your breakfast. I'm glad you stopped in today, Mason," she replied. "I have a feeling this is the start of something good for you and your dad."

"I hope so," Mason replied.

She patted him on the shoulder again and walked away.

"She's nice," I said when he didn't say anything.

He nodded.

I reached over and touched Mason's hand. I could see that he was still a little shaken by news.

"You okay?" I asked softly.

He nodded. "I just wish… I wish he would have tried
136

contacting me. Especially now that he's happy."

"Maybe he doesn't know how to contact you?" I offered.

"Or maybe I'm a part of his life he wants to forget."

"I doubt it, Mason. He might just be so ashamed of himself and his alcoholism," I said.

"I don't know. Maybe," he replied.

"Hopefully you'll find out."

He nodded. "I just wish I wasn't leaving in a few days. Even if she gives him my number, it doesn't mean he'll call."

My heart went out to him. "No, but at least he'll know you've been thinking about him."

He nodded slowly. "I guess."

While we ate, Mason told me a little more about his childhood and how he'd lost his mother. It had devastated him, especially when his father turned to alcohol to cope with everything. From what I understood, he was also the kind of man who became violent when he drank, so Mason had tried avoiding Len as much as possible.

"As soon as I graduated from high school I moved to California to try and make it as an actor. I did get a couple commercial roles, but nothing major, and eventually found a job at a coffee shop, which is how I met Zed."

"And the rest is history?" I asked, smiling.

He nodded. "It didn't happen overnight, though. It took a few years before we started getting real gigs. That was because of Mack, though."

"Your manager?"

"Yeah. We met him through Chance."

I furrowed my brow. "Chance? Coincidence?"

He chuckled. "No, my bandmate, Chance."

My cheeks heated. *Whoops.* "Which one is he?"

"Our keyboardist," he replied, looking amused.

I gave him a sheepish smile. "Sorry."

"No problem. I guess I should be happy you know who I am."

"And who is that again?" I teased.

Smiling, he flicked his straw at me.

I wiped the Coke from my cheek and smiled. "Don't start something you can't finish," I said, grabbing a small piece of ice and tossing it at him. "Remember the pillow fight?"

"I was going easy on you."

"I doubt it."

"Fine. We'll have a rematch. I won't hold back this time."

"Good." I stuck my tongue out at him for a split second.

He grinned.

Chapter 21
Mason

As we were leaving the diner, Terra called her mother and told her she was going to be there for dinner and that she was bringing a guest.

"He's *just* a friend," she said at one point during their conversation. As soon as I heard the words, I knew for sure that I wanted to be much more.

"So, what did your mom say?" I asked Terra after she hung up.

She shoved the phone into her purse. "She's excited I'm bringing someone over. She started asking me about you and, well, you heard. I didn't tell her much, which frustrated her. She hates being left in the dark."

"How should we tell her we met?" I asked.

"We'll tell her the truth. We met at the bakery."

I grinned. "Fair enough."

"Exactly. I just hope she doesn't recognize you."

"Does she listen to my music?"

"I'm sure she's heard you on the radio and would recognize one of your songs. As far as putting music and a face together, I doubt she'll figure it out. It's not like she watches videos or has an Instagram."

"Okay. Do you mind if we go back to my hotel so I can change?" I asked.

"No, but what if someone sees us sneaking in?"

I let out a ragged sigh. "I don't care. I'm done with sneaking around."

"What about the security guards? If they follow us to my mom's, the entire neighborhood might figure out who you are."

The thought made my blood boil. "They're not coming. I won't allow it."

She raised her eyebrow.

"I'm a grown man who pays their bills. I can put my foot down when I need to," I replied. It wasn't the security that worried me, however. It was Mack. If and when he found out, there'd be an argument. I didn't care, though. I could take care of myself. At least in Minnesota... where there wasn't a crazy stalker trying to kill me.

Smirking, she lay her head back against the seat. "This should be interesting."

Yeah, it should...

♥

We parked in the ramp and then took the elevator to my suite. Surprisingly enough, there weren't any security guards posted up in the hallway. It was unusual, considering how paranoid Mack was.

"Shit," I said, remembering I'd left the deadbolt on. "I'll have to sneak back in and unlock it from the inside."

"How are you going to do that?"

I explained that I'd rented the room below mine and had been using the balcony to get in and out.

Her eyes widened. "You crawled down from your suite? Isn't that dangerous?"

I shrugged. "A guy's gotta do what a guy's gotta do for a little freedom."

She laughed. "Apparently."

"I'll be right back. Wait here."

"Be careful."

The concern in her eyes disarmed me for a minute, so I did what every guy does and acted like I was an unbreakable superhero. "I'll be fine."

I turned and headed back down the hallway, took the stairs, and slipped into my other room. A few minutes later, I was in my main suite and unlocking the deadbolt. Opening the door, I was about to say something cocky when I saw that Terra wasn't alone. Mack and one of the security guards were talking to her.

"Hey, what's up?" I said, smiling at Mack.

"Where've you been all day?" he asked, his eyebrows furrowing.

"Around," I replied, grabbing Terra's hand and pulling her into my suite. "What about you?"

Mack's face looked stormy. "Don't be smartass. Why aren't you answering my texts and calls?" he asked.

"I've been having problems with my phone. Sorry," I lied.

He scowled. "That seems to be happening a lot lately. We should get it looked at."

He obviously knew I was bullshitting. "What do you need, Mack?"

He sighed. "We're leaving earlier than expected.

141

Tomorrow, in fact."

And he couldn't have just texted me that information? I frowned. "Why?"

"Some bullshit mix-up with the pilot's schedule."

"Sounds like an easy fix to me." I shrugged. "Get another pilot."

"Not enough time. Everyone wants to leave now, anyway," Mack replied.

I crossed my arms over my chest. "I don't."

"Well." He nodded toward Terra, "Obviously we know why. Bring her with."

Before I could say anything, Terra cut in. "I have a name. It's Terra. I'm not just an object. I can't just be moved or flown whenever it's convenient. I also don't like being ignored."

Mack had the decency to look embarrassed. "I apologize. I'm just stressed out."

"It's okay," she replied, relaxing.

He looked at me. "Look, I don't care who you bring, just be ready by eleven a.m. Meet us in the lobby."

I nodded.

"You staying in for the night?" Mack asked.

"Not sure," I replied.

"Let me know if you need protection," he replied.

I grunted. "It's in my wallet."

"I meant security, you smartass," he said, with a smirk.

"Sir, yes, sir," I said with a salute.

He gave me an annoyed loo, but before he could argue, I told him goodnight and then shut the door.

"I see what you mean," Terra said, walking to the fireplace. "About being babysat, I mean. It must be rough getting the third-degree all the time."

I ran a hand through my hair. "It is. It's definitely time for a change, though."

"A new manager?"

"A new… everything."

Chapter 22

Terra

I could see from his expression that he meant it, too.

"So, enough about my problems," he said quickly, before I could ask him any more questions. "What should I wear to your mother's? Is it a formal dinner?"

I laughed. "No, definitely not. Just casual."

"Okay." He took off his jacket and then his T-shirt, exposing his sexy muscular arms and lean abs again. I couldn't imagine what he'd think if he saw what I had hiding under my sweater. My abs were as soft as his were hard. If opposites really did attract, we were destined to be together forever.

"I'll be right out," he said, rolling his T-shirt into a ball.

I smiled weakly. "O… okay."

Mason disappeared into the bedroom and I walked back over to the piano. His sheet music was still sitting there and I started looking through it, unable to understand any of the notes, but still very curious. I sat down on the bench and started pressing some of the piano keys.

"Whatcha doin'?"

Startled, I looked up to find Mason standing behind me. He'd shaved and changed into a light blue fitted sweater that really brought out his piercing blue eyes. He looked even more handsome, if that were even possible.

I smiled shyly. "Just fooling around." I looked down at the keys and a wistful sigh slipped from my lips. "I've always wanted to learn to play the piano."

"I could teach you some things," he replied softly.

"That's very sweet of you, but I know you're short on time as it is," I replied.

"Let me show you a couple of things. Here," he said, leaning over my shoulder. "Let's start with the major keys and where they're located."

Inhaling his clean, masculine scent, I listened as he went over them and then showed me how to play some basic chords.

"Another thing, you have to make sure you hold your fingers like this," he said, his warm hands on mine as he showed me. "Otherwise, you could potentially have all kinds of problems later on down the line."

"You know, you promised me a song," I said, smiling.

He tried giving me a blank expression, but the sparkle in his eyes betrayed him. "What song?"

I snorted. "You're a bad liar. I think I'm finally catching on to you, Mr. Stone."

He grinned. "Is that so?"

"Sort of. Anyway, you told me you'd play one of the songs you've been working on. I've been dying to hear it."

He let out a sigh.

"Please? I've been waiting all day," I said more dramatically than I meant.

He bit back a smile. "Fine. But under one condition."

"What's that?" I asked, intrigued.

In answer, he slid his hand up to my cheek and stared into my eyes. "I get a kiss first," he whispered.

Were the rules changing?

"No," I said, even though I wanted nothing more.

His eyes widened. "No?"

I smiled, proud of my strength. "You can have one *after* you play."

Staring at my face, Mason caressed my cheek, and it gave me shivers.

"You're turning into a real ballbuster, aren't you?" he asked, his fingers slowly sliding up to my neck.

"I've always been a ballbuster," I breathed, my nipples tightening from his touch. "You're just getting to know *me* a little better now."

His eyes burned into mine. "I'd like to know you even more."

I swallowed and could do nothing but blink, as he'd rendered me speechless.

He removed his hand, grabbed the sheet music sitting on the piano, and began flipping through it.

I stood up and walked over to a painting on the wall. It was some kind of colorful abstract thing, but as an artist myself, I could appreciate its creativity.

"You can stay there," he replied, looking over at me.

"No. I'll stand. I need to stretch my legs out anyway."

The truth was, I didn't think we'd both fit comfortably on the small bench, and avoiding embarrassment was something I'd grown good at.

"Okay."

We switched spots and he sat down. Setting the sheet music back on the stand, he placed his fingers over the keys and began to play. It was a slow and rich melody, and as if watching his fingers play it wasn't mesmerizing enough, when he began to sing, my whole body became engulfed in goosebumps. Obviously I'd heard him sing before, but not this close up and personal, and certainly not when it was just the two of us.

Chapter 23

Mason

I felt anxious about singing her what I'd written. I'd kept all the new music to myself and hadn't even played any of it for the band or Mack. Not after being lectured about some of my older songs; apparently they weren't quite right for what the record producers wanted.

There were a few songs I was currently playing around with. The one I chose to sing to Terra was about love, loss, and heartbreak. Although one might expect the words to be about a woman, the inspiration came from losing both my parents. It was an emotionally-charged song, and I probably wouldn't have ever played it for Zed or the others, but I felt Terra would understand and appreciate it. From the tears glistening in her eyes as I sang the words, I'd been right.

"That was... incredible," she said on a sigh after I'd finished. "I'm just... I'm speechless."

"Thank you. It's about my parents."

Wiping away a couple tears that had spilled down her cheeks, she nodded. "That's immediately what I thought."

That pleasantly surprised me. "So... you liked it?"

She nodded emphatically. "Are you kidding me? I loved it. I'm overwhelmed with emotion right now. Obviously."

I grinned.

"I'll be honest, I really wasn't a fan before either. But, now.... I think I might be," she teased, trying to look serious. "You actually do have a little talent. Color me impressed."

Laughing, I stood up and walked over to her. "Does that mean I get more than one kiss?"

Her cheeks turned pink. "It depends on your breath. And mine. I'm just saying... we had a big breakfast and there were onions involved. Lots of them, especially in my omelet."

"Good thing I ate some of it. Now we both have onion breath." I slid my hands around her waist and pulled her against me. Feeling her body against mine gave me an instant woody.

"Maybe we should gargle with mouthwash before we have our first kiss?" she suggested, looking nervous.

"Maybe we shouldn't think too much about it," I replied leaning down and covering her lips with mine.

Terra

If either of us had bad breath, it wasn't noticeable. Hell, I was oblivious to everything but his tongue in my mouth, his arms around my waist, and the ache between my legs. Not only could the man sing like a dream, but he knew how to kiss a woman. He must have been enjoying himself, too, because I could feel his manhood pressing against me and it felt like a woman's version of a wet dream.

As the kiss continued, I could feel Mason's hands tighten as they gripped my sweater. Groaning, he pulled his face away from mine and stared down at me hungrily.

"If you wanted to kiss me twice, I wouldn't argue," I flirted with a little smile.

"I want to do more than that," he growled, running his hands over my back. "But..."

"But?"

"I'd sound like a hypocrite," Mason said, looking frustrated.

"You're not a hypocrite and I certainly wouldn't think that."

His eyes held mine. "I know what I want. What is it that you want?"

I swallowed. At that moment, I was so horny I wanted to tear his clothes off and ride him like a bull. "You. I mean, we can wait, but... we don't have to."

Mason stared at me with intensity, his jaw ticking as his eyes searched mine. "You sure?"

My answer was immediate. "Oh, hell, yeah I'm sure."

He crushed his lips against mine and pulled my sweater up far enough so he could slip his hands underneath. Starting with my lower back, he began caressing his way around until both hands were kneading my breasts. Soon my sweater was flying over my head and my bra was being unclasped. Tearing himself away from my mouth, he flinged my bra to the floor and leaned down, taking one of my nipples in his mouth.

Chapter 24

Mason

Her breasts were everything I'd dreamed about and more. They were round, heavy, and the kind women paid a fortune to try and imitate — only these were real... and all mine.

Trying not to lose control, I lowered my left hand to her beautiful ass and squeezed. She immediately reached down and touched the outline of my cock through my jeans. I knew right then that we needed to continue this in the bedroom.

"Come on," I said, taking her hand in mine.

Once in the bedroom, I pushed her down onto the bed, teased her nipples some more, and then proceeded to remove her leggings. Underneath she wore a black see-through thong which I thought was incredibly sexy. Especially on a full-figured woman with breasts and an ass a guy could sink his teeth into. I cupped her womanhood, and smiled as she gasped.

"You're so wet," I groaned, sliding a finger under the material and into her slick hole.

Terra moaned and began trying to grasp at the buttons on my jeans.

"Hold on," I whispered. "You touch me now and I'll never last. Just looking at you makes me want to explode."

She stared up at me with hunger and pressed her hand against the front of my jeans. "Can I at least see it?"

Knowing how badly she wanted me made it that much

harder to control. I quickly unbuttoned my jeans and pushed my Jockeys down. When she saw my hard cock, she tried grabbing at it again.

"Patience," I said, chuckling and patting her hand away. "Let me have some fun first."

Terra

Oh, my God, was he hung!

H.U.N.G.

His cock was at least eight inches, maybe more. So much bigger than Sonny's. I wanted it inside of me. I needed to feel it moving... stretching... filling me up.

"Patience," he whispered, pushing my greedy hand away. "Let me have some fun first."

"Don't be selfish," I teased.

With a wicked smile, he said, "I'll show you who's selfish." Pushing my knees apart, he shoved my panties to the side and began fingering me.

"Oh, God," I moaned as I grabbed the sheet and watched as he lowered his face between my legs. He pushed my lips apart with his slender fingers and began licking around my clit.

"Oh, my... Oh... God," I gasped as he began exploring my folds, his tongue driving me completely insane.

Smiling, he added his fingers, playing me like one of his instruments. The pressure inside of me grew with each stroke of his tongue and each thrust of his fingers, causing me to whimper and beg for release. Finally, when I didn't think I could take it anymore, the dam burst and I was rocked with an orgasm so fierce... I *was* the fat lady singing in the opera and loving every minute of it. Unabashedly, I cried out his name, God's name, and whoever else was listening.

"I guess that means I did it right," he joked with a deep chuckle, moving away from my trembling thighs a few seconds later.

Once I'd caught my breath, I gave him a lazy smile. "I'm sorry, when did you get here?"

Laughing, he nipped playfully at my thigh and then pulled his jeans off, his cock springing up hard, purple, and ready. I stared at him in all of his naked glory and it felt like I was dreaming.

Tattoos. A chiseled chest. Abs that looked like they'd never seen a single carb. A cock that was just like its owner—larger than life and hopefully just as talented. People would pay millions for this view of Mason Stone. And right now... he was one-hundred percent all mine...

Mason

After slipping on a condom, I crawled on top of Terra and couldn't help but immediately put my full attention back to her breasts. As my tongue and I were getting our fill, I felt her hand on my cock.

"Now, Mason," she ordered in my ear, her soft, warm had

moving to my balls and cupping them.

There was no fucking way I was going to last, which was why I'd gone down on her sweet heat right away. I'd never done that with strangers—especially not groupies. God knows where some of them had been. But Terra was special and needed special treatment. Watching her come had been sexier than hell and had almost put me over the edge. Just thinking about plunging into her wet pussy was making my dick throb.

Sitting up on my knees, I gripped her beautiful, fleshy hips and positioned myself against of her sweet, wet hole. As I stared down at her, I pushed inside, burying myself deep in her slippery, tight heat. Groaning in pleasure, I pulled back out and then slowly began pumping into her.

Fuck, I'll never last, I thought as she sheathed my cock perfectly.

"Faster," she begged huskily, her head arched back as her hips bucked in time with mine.

Gritting my teeth, I did as she asked, sliding in and out of her, one hand on her hip, the other rubbing her pussy again. Watching her breasts jiggle with each thrust, feeling her slippery tightness, and seeing the expression on her face as I fucked her was almost too much. Not wanting to come just yet, I pulled out and lay on my back as I flipped us around so she was now on top of me.

"Ride me," I commanded, reaching up and squeezing her breasts.

Terra smiled at my demand and impaled herself on my cock. She began making circular motions with her hips, the inner walls of her pussy massaging my cock as she moved.

"That's it," I whispered staring up at her. "Damn, you're

fucking beautiful. You going to come again for me, Sweet Cakes?"

Smiling down at me, the voluptuous beauty reached down and began to rub her clit.

Watching her masturbate with the help of my thickness turned me on. I grabbed her by the hips and began thrusting into her again, hard and fast.

"Yes... I'm coming..." Terra squeaked not too much later. Her hand stopped moving and she threw her head back and moaned.

Her tight pussy clenched up around my cock, and unable to hold back any longer, she milked the seed right out of me. Gasping for air from the way the orgasm had slammed out of me, I reached up and buried my face in her, soft, pillowy breasts, wishing I could stay there forever, it all felt so incredible. Eventually, I discarded the rubber and got back into bed with her. I pulled Terra into my arms and closed my eyes, exhausted from the lack of sleep from the previous night. Soon, we both fell asleep.

Chapter 25
Terra

It was Mason's cell phone that woke us up.

"It's Zed," he said, setting the phone down. "He still wants to do dinner. The guy is relentless. Unfortunately for him, I already have plans."

"You're avoiding him?" I asked.

"Yeah, I suppose I am. I'm just so tired of the same-old, same-old. After dinner, he usually wants to hit the bars and party until dawn. That's not me."

"You've grown up and he hasn't?" I asked rhetorically.

"Maybe," he said with a small smile.

"Oh, shit," I said, as I noticed the time on the nightstand clock. It was just past four, and I'd told my mother we'd be at her place by five.

"Don't worry. We have time," Mason murmured, putting his arms around me.

"No. I need to take a shower," I told him, pulling the sheet around me as I sat up. The smell of sex was all around us and my lady parts needed to be cleansed. "Do you mind?"

"Let's take one together," he suggested, pulling the sheet away from my chest. "And Terra... don't *ever* cover up my toys."

Laughing, I slapped his hand away from my chest. "We can play later when there's more time."

"I have to leave tomorrow, remember?" he pouted.

I sighed. "I know. We can leave my mother's place after dinner. I'll make up some excuse."

"You should come with." He was still lounging in bed, staring at me with a serious look on his beautifully handsome face.

I raised my eyebrow. "What?"

He sat up. "Fly with me to New York."

It sounded exciting, but I had too much to do at the bakery. "I really wish I could, but I have a business to run. I hate to admit I've never even been there."

"All the more reason to come with." He looked at me with a hopeful grin.

I smiled sadly. "I have some wedding cakes that need to be finished before the end of the week."

"Will they be done by Friday?"

"Hopefully by Thursday," I replied.

He grinned. "Perfect. I'll fly you out Thursday afternoon and will personally pick you up at the airport. We can spend the entire weekend together."

The thought of hanging out with him in New York sounded incredible. "Won't you be busy with the concert?"

"It won't be that bad. You can hang out backstage or I'll find you a seat up front on Friday night. Then on Saturday, I'll show you around New York City. We'll have a blast."

An opportunity like this didn't come around very often. I knew I'd be stupid not to take him up on the offer. Besides, I was already missing him and he hadn't even left yet.

I debated with myself before I nodded. "Well, okay."

Mason's eyes lit up. "Really?"

I grinned. "Yeah. But... as long as you meet me at the airport. I hate arriving in a new city and not knowing where to go." I smiled weakly and worried my lip, looking at him with sincerity. "I've actually had panic attacks before."

I told him about the experience I'd had when I went to Hollywood for the *Cake Queens* show. When I'd arrived at the airport, the driver assigned to pick me up hadn't been there. Not able to find him or get in touch with any of the show's producers, I'd started to panic. Especially after noticing some drugged-out looking creep had been following me through the airport. Fortunately, everything had turned out in the end, but it had convinced me to not ever travel alone again. But Mason was worth a little discomfort.

He stared at me with concern. "Don't worry, I'll be there. I'd never leave you stranded."

Somehow, even though we still barely knew each other, I believed him.

Chapter 26

Mason

After arguing with one of my security guards, we left the hotel without anyone trailing us, which was a relief. I knew Mack would be livid when he found out, but I wanted privacy and wasn't going to accept anything less.

When we arrived at Terra's mother's dinner party, there were seven people gathered around the living room—her mother's sister Marcella, Jackie, who I'd learned was her mother's partner, Jackie's nephew, Tyler, and his date. And an older couple who lived across the street, Hank and Ethel. The neighborhood was located in Minneapolis, in a quiet part of town where the houses were older, but kept up, and everyone must have spent a lot of time gardening. It was definitely a retirement type community.

When we first walked in, Terra introduced me to her mother, Maria, as Mason and left it at that. Fortunately, nobody seemed to recognize me, which was a relief. But then Maria asked about my career.

"Mom," scolded Terra. "That's kind of personal."

"What's personal about asking what someone does for a living?" she replied, holding her hands out. "Sheesh, I ask one question and I'm already getting into trouble."

"It's okay," I replied, feeling the tension rise. I didn't want to be the cause of an argument and decided to give some kind of an answer. "I'm a writer."

"Oh? What kind of a writer? A journalist?" she asked.

"Actually, I'm a composer," I replied.

"That's intriguing," Jackie said. "You write songs. What kind?"

"Mostly rock," I replied.

"Do you get paid for it?" Maria asked.

"Oh, my God," Terra huffed. "Why don't you just ask him what his net worth is?"

"Relax," Maria replied, frowning. "I'm just asking questions. Frankly, I find it fascinating that Mason writes music, and if he's getting paid for it, more power to him."

"I'm not getting paid right now for the ones I've written. But, I'm hoping it will change soon," I said.

"You should play one for us," Tyler said, speaking up for the first time. "I saw a piano in the living room. I'm sure we'd all love to hear something you've written."

"Mason is here to relax," Terra said with a strained smile. "I'm sure that's the last thing he feels like doing right now."

"If you change your mind, we'd love to hear you play," Maria said.

I chuckled.

I hadn't said 'no'. In fact, I wasn't sure how I felt about hiding who I was anymore. Especially after what had happened between us back at the hotel. If we were going to go any further, her mother deserved to know the truth, at the very least. I decided to wait until the end of the evening and see how it went. If I felt comfortable enough, I'd play a song before we took off.

"Thank you," I said. "I'll think about it. My voice is a little hoarse today. You might not want to hear me sing."

"It can't be worse than mine," Tyler said. "When I sing, I sound like a cat in heat. Or one that's been hit by a bus.

Regardless, my voice is hard on the ears."

"That's not always bad. In fact, some of the up-and-coming artists sound pretty hellish," I replied. "These days, it's all about sounding different and making a statement. Carrying a note doesn't seem to matter as much anymore."

"I've noticed," Jackie said. "Some of the crap they play on the radio is atrocious."

"Speaking of the radio," Tyler's date, Angie, said as she stared at me. "Has anyone ever told you that you look like the lead singer from *My Life In Chaos*?"

Terra gave me a wide-eyed look.

"I've been told that I look like a lot of people," I replied.

"I bet him more than anyone, though," Angie replied. "I should look him up on my phone."

It was definitely time to change the subject and I was hungry. Whatever was in the oven smelled delicious. "By the way, what's that wonderful smell?"

Before she could answer, a long, drawn-out fart erupted somewhere by Hank and Ethel. From the expression on Hank's face, he hadn't noticed, but Ethel looked horrified.

"Sorry," Ethel said, blushing. "He does that sometimes and doesn't always realize it. I think his hearing aid is going bad, too."

"I'm surprised he didn't feel it," Marcella said, chuckling. "I did all the way over here."

We all laughed.

"Everyone is laughing. What'd she say?" Hank asked, putting his finger in his ear. "Let me turn up my hearing aid."

"It's okay, Hank. They were talking about dinner," she said, patting his hand.

"Oh, yes. It smells very good. What are we having?" Hank asked.

Maria smiled. "It's lasagna. An old family recipe."

"It really does smell amazing," I said. "I can't wait to try it out."

Fortunately, the conversation shifted once again and eventually Maria made an announcement, which apparently was the reason for the dinner party.

"Jackie and I are getting married," she told everyone, her eyes sparkling. "We'd like to do it somewhere in the Caribbean, we're just not sure where yet. We hope some of you can join us."

"What did she say?" Hank asked, fiddling with his hearing aid again.

"They're getting married!" Ethel hollered.

"Who?" he asked.

"Maria and Jackie," she replied.

He smiled. "That's great. When do we get to meet their future husbands?"

"No, Hank. *They* are getting married. To each other," she said.

A confused look crossed his face but then he smiled. "I'm very happy for you both." Then he looked at me. "Wouldn't you love to be a fly on the wall on *their* wedding night?" He wiggled his tongue back and forth.

I couldn't help but laugh. The old man was a riot.

Maria snorted and shook her head.

"I'm sorry, Maria." Ethel scowled at him and swatted his shoulder. "Watch your manners."

"Relax, woman. It's the eighties. Quit being so uptight," he grumbled.

"It's not the eighties, Hank," his wife replied, looking tired. "It's you who's in your eighties. And soon, I will be, too."

Hank sighed and looked over at me. "Life goes by in a blink of the eye. You should marry Terra now and start having kids."

"They're not a couple, Hank," Ethel said. "Just friends."

"We thought Jackie and Maria were just friends, too, and look at what happened." He wiggled his eyebrows. "Bow-chicka-bow-wow," he sang.

Ethel put a hand on her forehead. "I'm sorry."

"Nothing to be sorry for," Maria said, smiling. "It's just Hank being Hank. It's why we love him."

"I could actually listen to him all day. I bet Hank could teach me a lot," I said, chuckling.

The old man farted again.

Everyone laughed.

"Hank, what have you been eating?" Ethel said, waving her hand in front of her face.

"It's *your* cooking that gave me gas," he replied. "*You* should be the one to apologize for it."

The man cracked me up. I hoped to be like him when I grew up.

"Maybe I should become a lesbian. I seem to scare men away," Marcella said suddenly out of the blue.

"Are you even interested in women?" Maria asked her sister.

"If you mean sexually, no. I would like a companion, though," she replied and smirked. "One that doesn't have four legs or sound like Tyler when in heat."

We laughed.

"You should join the dating service we used to find each other," Tyler said, grabbing Angela's hand. "They match you up with people who fit your personality."

Marcella burst out laughing. "Now why would I want an asshole like me?"

"You are *not* an asshole," Maria replied, looking amused. "You're just very upfront about things."

"Plus, I swear like a sailor," she answered. "And dammit to hell if I want some motherfucker adding to it."

Terra had been right. Her family was non-conventional, and I loved it.

Through the course of the evening, I started to get used to the occasional cursing from Marcella, the bickering between Terra and her mother, and the occasional farts from Hank. In fact, they all made me feel welcomed to the point that I decided to play the song if they asked again.

"We should get going," Ethel said, after we finished dessert, a three-layer banana-split cake her mother had made. Apparently, Terra wasn't the only one with skills, because I couldn't stop eating it. "I hate to eat and run, but you know us. Early to bed and early to rise."

"It's okay, Ethel," Maria said.

"The food was delicious," Hank said. "You always outdo yourself."

164

Maria smiled. "You're so sweet. Thank you."

My cell phone buzzed. I checked to find it was Mack. Obviously, he wasn't happy, but demanded I check in with him when I arrived back at the hotel to make sure that I'd made it back safely. I told him I would and left it at that.

"Your babysitter again?" Terra asked.

I shoved my phone back into my pocket. "Yeah."

"Is he freaking out?"

"Nah. He's fine."

"Good."

As the older couple prepared to leave, Terra whispered that we should get going, too.

"Okay," I replied.

She told Maria that we were also planning on leaving and that's when Tyler mentioned the song.

"There's no time. We really need to go. I have to work early," Terra said, looking irritated that he was asking me about it again.

"That's too bad. We were really looking forward to you playing something," Maria said, listening in.

"Next time, maybe," Terra replied, giving me an "I'm Sorry" look.

"Does that mean you two are dating?" Maria asked, a hopeful expression on her face.

Amused that I was being left out of the conversation again, I cut in before Terra could answer.

I cleared my throat. "Yes. It means we're dating and that I *will* be back."

Terra stared at me wide-eyed.

"I just don't know when it will be, so if you really *want* to hear a song, I can play one right now," I added. "As long as Terra is okay with it."

Terra moved close to me. "Are you sure?" she whispered.

I nodded. "Yeah. After all, if I can't be honest with your family, I shouldn't even be here."

She smiled.

Chapter 27
Terra

'd been ready to chastise my mother about being nosy again when Mason not only told her that we were dating, but relented about the song. I'm not sure why he'd caved, especially since they'd figure out he was more than just a composer once he started singing. Admittedly, part of me was excited to hear him do it and see their reactions. I loved his voice and was beginning to really have strong feelings for the man attached to it.

We all filed into the living room, including Ethel and Hank, who'd decided to stick around a little longer. Mason sat down in front of the piano, an old Steinway upright which hadn't been used in ages. My father had played occasionally, which is why she'd kept it. More than once she'd made comments about her grandchildren taking lessons, which meant my kids, since I was her only child.

Mason began testing the keys, and as he did, I wondered what he was going to play, since he didn't have sheet music with him. It didn't take long before I realized he'd memorized the song he'd sung for me earlier.

As he played it, everyone stared in total silence, the shock on their faces very apparent. All except for the old couple, who smiled and nodded as he sang. They had no idea who he was, which was actually kind of sweet.

When it was over, everyone clapped and gushed over the song.

"Am I missing something here? Because you *really* sound like the guy I was talking about earlier. The one from *My Life*

In Chaos," Angie said, still looking confused and a little suspicious.

"The songs you hear on the radio are not mine, but... I *am* forced to sing them," Mason replied with a smile.

The room became silent.

"So, you really are Mason Stone?" Jackie said, pointing at him, her mouth slightly hanging open.

He nodded.

"Didn't I tell you?" my mother said with a victorious grin. "And you thought that I was crazy."

"I was wrong and you were right. For once," Jackie replied to her, but winking at Mason.

I stared at my mother in shock. "You'd already figured it out?"

"Oh... for Heaven's sake. His name is Mason. He said he was a composer. I'm certainly not blind and have seen him in magazines and on television. It couldn't have been anymore clearer if he'd have worn a nametag," she replied dryly. "I just don't understand why you didn't tell us."

"It's my fault," Mason said with an apologetic grin. "I wanted to get to know you as a regular person and not...well, you know. Someone like me."

"A regular person?" repeated Marcella with a snort. "What, when you become a celebrity you're above being regular?"

His eyes widened. "No. I didn't mean it like that. It's just—"

"I'm only giving you crap, dammit to hell," Marcella said, laughing. "We understand. You don't want to be treated special."

"Yes, thank you," Mason said, looking relieved. "I don't like to think of myself as better than anyone, but once you're on the radio, people treat you differently. Fame is really not all it's cracked up to be."

"A lot of people love the attention, though," Tyler said. "And the adoring fans."

"Don't get me wrong, I appreciate my fans. I just want a normal life sometimes," he replied.

Tyler held his hand out. "As a 'normal' guy, I can't say that I *wouldn't* switch lives with you in a heartbeat, but I respect what you're saying."

Mason shook his hand. "Thank you. Can I just say that your teeth are amazingly white?"

Tyler chuckled. "I'm a dentist and yes, they've been bleached."

"I'd get mine done, but I'm afraid they'd glow up on the stage," Mason joked.

Tyler squinted at Mason's mouth, and then pulled out a business card and held it out to him. "Your teeth look pretty good from where I'm standing, but if you want to make an appointment for a consultation, call my office tomorrow."

"Thanks. I'm leaving on a plane tomorrow. But maybe next time I'm in the cities," he replied, tucking the card into his pants pocket.

As far as I could tell, Mason's teeth were as perfect as the rest of him. I had a feeling that he was just being nice.

"Sounds good," Tyler said.

"We should go," Mason said, looking at me.

"Wait, can I get a selfie? Pretty please?" Angie asked and then gave an embarrassed look. "I'm sorry, is that tacky of me to ask? Especially after what you just said?"

"It's fine," Mason replied. "Now, if you were to try taking a glass, with my DNA on it to sell on eBay, then I might get a little offended."

We all laughed.

"How much do you think we could get for something like that?" Marcella asked.

I glared at her, ready to scold her.

Her face broke into a smile. "Oh, relax, motherfuckers. I'm just kidding."

Chapter 28

Mason

After we returned to the hotel, I sent Mack a text informing him that I'd returned. He thanked me and then reminded me again about leaving the next day.

"I should get going," Terra said, looking sad. "It's getting late and I have to be at the bakery by six."

"Can't you stay the night?" I asked, giving her a pouty face. "We won't see each other until Thursday. I'll make sure you're up in time to get to work."

Smiling, she relented.

We made love and then I held her in my arms, happy and content. I didn't know where things were going, and we barely knew each other, but the woman was already getting under my skin. I hadn't even left yet and I was already counting the days until I'd see her again.

It was still dark outside when I woke Terra up at five.

"Damn, *already*?" she groaned and then yawned.

"Yeah. You should hire someone to open in the morning for you."

"I'm baking in the morning. Not just opening."

"Can't someone else do it?"

"I suppose. It would take time to hire someone and train them in properly, though."

"If you did, we could spend more time together after I'm done touring, then."

"When will that be?"

"Another month and I'll have a free schedule for a while."

Her face brightened. "Really?"

"Yeah. I'll fly you out to California when it's over. You can see my place."

I told her about my house, which was in the heart of Beverly Hills. A decent sized mansion with a swimming pool and a basketball court.

"It sounds amazing," she replied.

"It's nice. Not as glamorous as a lot of other houses in the area. But, I'm a bachelor and I have everything I need."

"Do you have any pictures?"

I pulled out my phone and showed her the pictures of my kitchen. "I don't have any pictures of the rest of the house, sorry."

"It's okay. The kitchen looks really nice."

"Thanks. I just had it remodeled. I'm happy with it and I hope you like it, not that I expect you to cook for me. I have a personal chef on call."

"Are you kidding? I'd *love* to cook for you," Terra replied.

I grinned. "Good. Then it's settled. Once you find someone to help you with the bakery, you can come out and visit."

Her smile fell. "Even if I do hire someone, I can't just leave for days on end. It's my business. My cakes. My reputation."

"Then I'll come to you. Who knows, maybe I'll even move back here."

Her eyebrows shot up. "Really? You'd do that?"

172

"Maybe. We'll see how things go," I replied. "I seriously wouldn't mind moving back to Minneapolis, though."

She gave me a pensive look.

"What's wrong?"

"Nothing. It's just that… you wanted to take things slowly and now you're making these plans already."

"I know. I never expected this to happen so soon. I also never expected to want you so much."

Her eyes filled with pleasure. "You still do? Even after you've already had me?"

"More so now because of it." I pulled her against me. "Sweet Cakes, I'm going to miss the hell out of you."

"I'll miss you, too. I hope you'll call me tonight."

"Of course. As soon as I arrive in New York and am at my hotel, masturbating and thinking of your fun bags. By the way, can I take a picture of you naked?"

Terra gasped. "No."

"I won't share it with anyone. Please?"

She gave me a little smile. "I'll think about it."

Chapter 29

Terra

A s I drove home, I couldn't wipe the smile off of my face. The man was incredible and I couldn't believe he was actually contemplating moving back to Minnesota.

Turning on the radio, one of his songs came on and I quickly raised the volume. Now, every word he sang felt like it was directed toward me. Of course, I knew it wasn't really, but it was fun pretending.

I stopped home, took a quick shower, and headed off to Sweet Treats, arriving a little later than I'd wanted to. As I worked on the first cake, I started thinking about what Mason had suggested and decided that hiring another baker might not be such a bad idea. Especially if we were going to be spending more time together.

"Oh, my God," gushed Cindy when she stepped into the shop, a couple hours later. "I heard about you and Mason Stone. Why didn't you tell me?"

Staring at her, I asked how she'd found out.

"I saw it on *My Life In Chaos*'s Facebook page... at the pre-party. There was a video they shared of the two of you, moving toward the stage. The host of Hollywood Star Tracker was talking about Mason Stone's mysterious woman. Of course, I recognized you right away."

I giggled.

"So, that *was* him in the bakery the other day, wasn't it?"

"Yes, but I didn't know until that night."

"Did you guys hook up? I heard he's great in bed."

I wasn't about to tell her if we had sex or not. "How did you hear that he's great in bed?"

"I read it in some magazine. Some supermodel said he was the best she'd ever had."

"Ah."

"Obviously, you two are just friends. I mean, he dates celebrities and models. I'm sure he wouldn't date me either, let alone you."

I knew she wasn't trying to be rude on purpose, but her words cut me. Mostly because I recognized the look in her eyes. She thought we were just friends because of my size.

"Actually, we did get together," I said, my pride getting the best of me.

Her eyes grew wild. "You did?"

"Yeah. Just, don't tell anyone."

She rushed over and grabbed my arm. "Oh, my God, what was it like? It must have been incredible."

I smiled. "Let's just say that he is a very attentive lover."

Cindy gave me a strange look again and I knew she was still having a hard time believing me.

I cleared my throat and nodded toward the showroom. "You should probably see if Marcella needs any help up front," I said, looking back at my cake. "It's about to get busy soon, too."

"Yeah. Okay."

A few hours later, Mason called me from New York City. We talked for a short time and then he informed me that he'd already paid for my ticket on Thursday.

"I'll send you the ticket information," he said.

"Okay. Thanks."

"I miss you, Sweet Cakes," Mason said.

I smiled. "I miss you, too."

"Have you thought about what we talked about earlier?"

"What's that? Hiring someone else for the bakery?"

"I meant the nude pic of you," he said, a smile in his voice.

"I don't know," I replied, looking down at myself. The idea of sending him a nude picture was kind of exciting, but it was risky, too. I wasn't a risky woman. At least, I never used to be.

"You're just so beautiful and I can't stop thinking about you."

"Tell you what, if you send me one of you, I'll send you one of me," I replied. "But, *you* first."

He went silent.

"Hello?" I said.

"You won't show anyone?"

"No. Of course not."

"If it got out…"

"You don't trust me?"

"It's not that I don't trust you. I'm just worried your

176

phone might fall into the wrong hands."

I understood his concern. I felt the same way, which was really the only thing holding me back from sending one to him. "I understand."

"You're still sending me one though, right?"

I frowned. "No. I don't want my picture getting out, either."

"I won't show anyone. I promise."

"If you're not sending one of yourself, then I'm not sending one either," I said, feeling defiant.

He sighed.

"Terra, you have a call on Line One," Cindy called into the back room.

"I have to go," I said to Mason.

"Okay," he said in a pouty voice. "Call me later when you can."

"I'll call you when I get home from work, okay?"

"Sounds good."

Later that night, before calling him back, I took off my clothes and stared at my reflection in the full-length mirror. After mulling over the nude photo request all day, I'd decided to send him one. It was unfair of me to think that my picture could be as damaging as his, if it were to actually get out into the public.

Sucking in my stomach, I posed for a couple of selfies and

then went over the pictures.

"Yuck. Yuck. No way. Eh.... Not going to happen."

After about fifty more poses, I decided on one that wasn't too bad, and in fact, actually made me look a little sexy.

I sent Mason a text.

Me: *You around?*

A few seconds later, he answered my text. *Yeah, I just finished my dinner. You done working?*

Me: *Yes. Are you alone?*

Mason: *Of course.*

I sent him the photo.

A few seconds later he sent me a smiling devil emoji.

Mason: *Hot damn, you look sexy.*

Me: *Thanks.*

Mason: *No bush shot?*

I sent him an angry emoji face.

Mason: *LOL*

I asked him how his day had gone and it took him awhile to respond.

Mason: *Crappy. I have jet-lag and feel sleepy.*

Me: *Bummer. I wish I was with you right now.*

Mason: *So do I.*

A photo from him popped up and it made me gasp and then laugh. It was of his erect penis and he'd constructed a miniature pair of paper sunglasses and had somehow stuck them onto the tip.

Mason: *Incognito.*

Me: *LOL. How did you get the sunglasses to stick?*

Mason: *Tape.*

Me: *Ouch. That's going to leave a mark.*

Mason: *Don't worry, I'm a professional!*

We texted for about an hour and then he told me that he was drifting off. We told each other goodnight and then I plugged my phone into the charger, feeling giddy and excited about seeing him in a few days. As I was thinking about what to take on the trip, my phone rang. It was Celine.

"Terrabae, how've you been?" she asked. "I feel like we haven't talked in ages."

"Wonderful."

"*Wonderful?* Okay. Spill it. Nobody says wonderful the way you just did unless they've gotten laid."

I told her about Mason and what had happened over the last couple of days.

"And you didn't call me? Your best friend? The one who brought you two together?"

She had a point. If it wasn't for the concert, I didn't know if things would have progressed the way they had. I apologized and told her about New York.

She squealed. "No wonder you're so happy! You must feel like a princess who's been swept off of her feet."

In a way, I did.

"Just be careful," Celine said. "Remember what they say about him in the tabloids. He's a womanizer."

"I think that's just made up. The Mason I know doesn't seem like that. In fact, he hates it when women chase him."

"Because they do it all the time. No wonder why he hates

it. That doesn't mean he's not going to chase other women, though."

I sighed. I would have said the same things to her if the tables were turned. But she didn't know Mason like I did.

"There's have nothing to worry about."

She groaned. "I just don't want you getting your heart broken again."

"I'm not in love with the guy. We're just having fun."

"I know you better than anyone. You're already thinking about making changes in your life for him, aren't you?"

Damn, she definitely knew me.

"I'll be fine," I promised.

"I hope so. Just don't expect him to be the kind of Prince Charming you see in the movies. Real life isn't like that. Especially the rich and famous. They take, take, take. You're the kind of woman who gives, gives, gives. It worries me."

"So, you think that I should just give up on the guy already?"

"No. Just... keep your eyes open, and don't be naïve."

I gritted my teeth. "I've never been naïve, Celine."

She sighed. "So, when did you say you were going out to New York City?"

"Thursday. He bought me a ticket."

"If I were you, I'd show up a day earlier. Surprise him. If he's doing something wrong, you'll know."

"Doing something wrong? You really don't trust Mason, do you?"

"You're my best friend. I don't trust anyone with your

180

heart until they've proven themselves," she said softly.

I smiled. "That's why I love you, Celine. You keep things in perspective for me every damn time."

"Exactly. Which is why I think you should go to New York on Wednesday and surprise him."

"But... I trust him."

"That's what you said about Sonny, once."

"Sonny was different."

"Yeah, he was. Sonny was a homely, boring, selfish jerk. Mason is a gorgeous, rich, sought-after hottie."

She had a point...

Chapter 30

Mason

ⁿ On Tuesday, I called and spoke to Terra before meeting up with the band for rehearsal. She sounded a little distant, but blamed it on having went in to work earlier.

"I've been here since three-thirty," she said, in a tired voice.

"Why so early?"

"To get these cakes finished. I was hoping to maybe even finish by tomorrow."

"Don't beat yourself up, though. I know you want to finish them but you should get some rest, too."

"I'll rest when I'm dead," she joked.

I chuckled. "I hear you."

"So, what are you up to today?" she asked.

"Rehearsal and then I'm meeting up with Zondra," I said.

"Oh, isn't that the lead singer of The Sun Chasers?"

"Yeah. We're having dinner at Peter Luger Steak House."

She gasped. "Peter-freaken-Lugers? No way. I've always wanted to eat at that place."

"I'll take you there sometime."

"I would love that."

"Maybe I can get us in later in the week."

"If you can't, you can't. No biggie. So… is Zondra nice?"

she asked lightly.

"Yeah, she's a sweetheart."

"And you two are just friends?"

I chuckled. "Of course. We work together and she's an amazing woman. We're *not* romantically involved, I assure you."

"So, you never dated?"

I told her the truth. "A long time ago, we went out a few times. It didn't work out."

I almost thought she was going to ask me if we'd had sex, and I would have had to answer 'yes', but fortunately, she didn't.

"She's beautiful."

"Yeah. You're beautiful, too. Which is why I can't stop looking at the picture you sent," I said, wanting to change the subject. I knew she was anxious about Zondra because of what her ex had done to her. She'd confided in me the night before and I found out that it had taken her months to get over.

"Make sure you don't show anyone," she said.

"Of course I wouldn't. I don't want anyone seeing my toys. They'll try and borrow them. I don't like sharing."

She laughed.

"Anyway," I looked at the clock, "I have to get going so I'm not late. I just wanted to call and see how you were."

"Okay."

I pictured her beautiful face and sighed. "I can't wait to see you."

"I can't wait to see you, either."

We made plans to talk later in the evening and then we both hung up.

Terra

I was jealous. I couldn't help it.

Knowing that he was going to dinner with Zondra made me anxious. If they'd dated, they'd probably had sex, too. Both of them were so damn beautiful, I couldn't imagine them *not*.

I tried not to think about Mason and Zondra for the rest of the day, but it was hard. All I kept thinking about was the woman's cute little shape and it made me want to stop eating completely. I'd actually lost most of my appetite, despite going back on the Keto diet, and I attributed it to my growing feelings for Mason. Every time I thought of him, my heart soared and my stomach felt like it was caging a swarm of restless butterflies.

When I finally left the bakery, it was almost nine o'clock at night. Exhausted, hungry, and still very much anxious about Zondra and Mason, I stopped at Taco Bell, which wasn't on my diet plan. I ordered some comfort food, brought it home, and pigged out. When I was finished, I felt disgusted with myself for being so weak. As I was throwing the empty bag away, I spotted my laptop and decided to log into my diet website

I perused around the *Curvy Hips and Sexy Lips* site and found one of the message boards entitled, *Slip-ups and Cheats: It's Not The End Of the World*. I clicked on it.

I knew full well I was on here because misery loves company, and I was clearly not alone. From just today alone, there were over a hundred posts from women who'd slipped up and given in to temptation, or were on vacation and didn't care, or ones who were going through a hard time and had taken to eating comfort food. They admitted it hadn't really helped, and reminded themselves that tomorrow was another day.

While I wasn't exactly devastated by the fact I'd eaten fast food, it did make me feel better that I wasn't alone, and that yes, tomorrow was another day to start fresh.

As I began to click around to find my Keto board to find some new recipes, my phone chimed.

Mason: *Just want you to know that I'm thinking about you.*

I sent him a heart.

Me: *Are you finished with dinner?*

Mason: *Yeah. Zondra and I are meeting Zed and Palmer at a club in a few. She's depressed and needs company.*

I wanted to ask what was wrong, but didn't want to push it. Plus, I felt like I was starting to sound like my nosy mother.

Me: *Okay. Have fun. Call me later if you want.*

Mason: *I'll try. It might be really late.*

Me: *I don't care.*

Mason. *Sleep well.*

Me: *Thanks.*

185

Sighing, I put my phone away and then took a shower. After getting my pajamas on, I went into the bedroom and read until my eyelids grew too heavy to stay open. Checking the time, I decided to just go to bed. It was after eleven and I wanted to get to the bakery early and finish the last cake. If I worked diligently enough, I'd get it done before noon. An entire day earlier than I'd originally planned.

My alarm jolted me awake at three-thirty. I shut it off at the same time I realized that Mason hadn't called me back. Grabbing my phone from the nightstand, I checked to see if there was a text or I'd somehow missed his call. There was nothing.

Fighting the urge to contact him, I told myself that he was probably sound asleep in his hotel room and that although it was three-thirty here, it was four-thirty in New York. Calling him at this hour would make me look like a jealous girlfriend checking up on a man she didn't trust. Two reasons kept me from doing it: One, he hadn't given me a motive to *not* trust him. Two, I wasn't his girlfriend.

But, we were dating, I reminded myself. *That had to mean something.*

It meant that I'd better figure out what the hell I was getting myself into before I *did* get hurt.

Chapter 31

Mason

Somehow, during the time we'd met up with Zed and Palmer, I'd lost my goddamn cell phone.

"So, you're telling me that someone is going through your phone and looking through all your dirty pictures?" Zed said, looking amused.

"We're talking about *my* phone. Not yours. I could imagine the filthy shit you have on your camera roll," I replied.

"It's true. He has a lot of incriminating shit on his phone," Palmer said, smirking. "Stuff that involves furry creatures."

Zed gave him the finger.

"I was talking about your ex Darla," laughed Palmer. "The one with the goatee."

Zed flipped him off with both middle fingers.

"Mason, call your cell provider. They can probably locate it for you," Zondra said, ignoring them.

I sighed in relief. "Good idea."

She loaned me her phone and I called, but it didn't do much good. Unfortunately, there was some app I'd never downloaded, which could have helped us locate the phone.

"We'll flag your phone as lost. You'll want to change all of your passwords by logging into your account..." the woman droned on and on, telling me how to do it.

"What's going to happen to the items on my phone? You

know, all of the pictures and stuff?"

"It can be extracted and saved," she replied.

I relaxed.

After hanging up, I handed Zondra her phone back.

"It sucks, doesn't it?" she said. "I'd almost rather lose my purse than my phone. We rely on these things so much."

"Too much," I muttered.

What really irritated me was that I hadn't memorized Terra's cell phone number and didn't know her home one either. I'd have to wait and call her in the morning at *Sweet Treats*. When she found out that I'd lost my phone, she wasn't going to be happy, either. I'd promised to keep the naked picture of her safe and I couldn't even get that right. Her aunt was right. I really was a motherfucker.

We finally made it back to our hotel around two. The four of us had fun, despite me losing my phone. Fortunately, Zondra, who was going through a messy divorce, had been able to relax and forget about the bad shit in her life for a while.

"Thanks for walking me to my door," Zondra said as she unlocked her room. "And for the wonderful night."

"It was my pleasure."

She turned around and smiled up at me. "Did you want to come in for a drink?"

I'd already had more than I should have. I wasn't drunk, but not feeling much pain either. "It's late. I should probably go."

"You can sleep in my bed tonight. You know… like old times?" she said softly.

We'd had sex twice, and admittedly, it had been pretty amazing. Still, it was nothing compared to what I'd experienced with Terra. Had things been different, I might have taken her up on the offer. But there was a new woman in my life. A good one. One who'd already had her heart broken in the last year. I wasn't going to do anything that might hurt her again.

"As enticing as that sounds, I can't. I told you about Terra," I replied.

"Ah, that's right. Little Betty Crocker," she replied, crossing her arms under her chest. "She must do her best cooking under the sheets, huh?"

I chuckled. "It's more than that. I don't know, there's just something about her. I can't get her out of my mind. I'm even flying her out here on Thursday."

She studied me closely and smirked. "Why, Mason Stone… are you falling in love?"

Was I?

I'd never been in love before, but I felt something for Terra. Something… pretty damn intense. "Maybe. It's probably too early to tell. We just met."

"Don't ever let anyone tell you that there's no such thing as love at first sight. There is. My parents experienced it and are still going strong after thirty-five years."

"Really?"

She smiled bitterly. "Yeah, it actually happened to me, too. I fell in love with Byron immediately. I really thought he'd loved me the same way, too. But, I don't think he knows what true love is."

"I'm sorry," I said, wishing her only happiness. From what I'd learned of her ex, he had a lot of mistrust issues. "There'll be someone else. Someone who will make you happy and be the kind of guy you deserve. Someone much better than Byron."

"Yeah. I know." She sighed wearily. "Well, I'm tired, and since you're not coming in, you should probably get some rest, too."

"Did you want to grab breakfast tomorrow?" I asked.

"I'll let you know," she replied, a distant look in her eyes.

I frowned. "Are you okay?"

Her smile seemed forced. "I'm fine, considering the situation. Just so damn tired, you know?"

"I hear you. A good night's sleep will hopefully help."

She nodded.

We hugged, and then, with my security entourage in tow, I headed to my hotel room to also get some sleep.

As I lay in bed, I felt a little down, knowing that I couldn't get in touch with Terra. I'd been getting used to talking to her before bed, and now I found that I actually *needed* to hear her voice. Unfortunately, I had a feeling she was going to be a little upset, especially after telling her about Zondra. I didn't want her to feel jealous, but knew if the tables were turned, I'd be on a flight to New York by now. Jealousy wasn't usually a problem for me, but with Terra it was different. I was already feeling protective and possessive. Even the thought of Zed talking about her breasts irritated me. Closing my eyes, I drifted off to sleep, reminding myself that she'd be there soon and in my arms.

I WOKE UP to the shrill sound of the hotel's phone ringing off of the hook. Looking at the clock, I saw it was just past four a.m. Worried that it might be Terra, I quickly picked it up.

"Hey, it's Mack. I'm sorry for calling you so late, but... it's Zondra."

"What about her?" I asked, suddenly fully awake.

He paused. "She's dead, Mason. I'm sorry."

Chapter 32

Terra

When I didn't hear from Mason by eight a.m., I sent him a text asking how his night went. He didn't answer me, so I assumed that he was probably still sleeping. I just hoped it was by himself.

Sighing, I went back to work on the wedding cake for a couple who wanted a Hawaiian Theme. They'd eloped in Maui the week before, and were now having a surprise reception, thrown by the couple's parents. As I was adding some pink and white hibiscus flowers, my cell phone rang. Oddly enough, it was my mother, who never called me in the mornings.

"Have you seen the news?" she asked quickly.

"No. Why?"

"A woman died last night. In New York."

"Okay...?"

"Her name was Zondra Phillips."

The blood rushed to my ears. "What?"

"She was either pushed or leaped out of her hotel balcony. Apparently, one of the last people she was seen with beforehand was Mason Stone."

My jaw dropped. "You're kidding?"

"No. It's all over the news. Mason's been brought in for questioning."

I felt physically ill.

Poor, beautiful Zondra.

I couldn't imagine that someone with so much would commit suicide. But, there was no way in hell I believed Mason had anything to do with it. "He was not involved with this," I said, my eyes filling with tears. "Mason would never hurt her."

"Let's hope not. He seems like such a nice young man."

"He is, Mom. He is."

After hanging up with her, I felt helpless and needed to talk my best friend. She was my rock and always gave me strength.

"I'm sorry, but I knew there was something off about that man," Celine said angrily. "Now that poor woman is dead."

My eyes widened. I hadn't expected her to accuse him of killing Zondra.

"He had *nothing* to do with her death," I protested angrily.

"You don't know. They had dinner together and you said he never called you back. Well, now... we know why. He probably killed her and had other things on his mind."

Leave it to Celine and her wild imagination. I just couldn't believe that Mason was responsible. In my heart, I *knew* he wasn't.

"Mason told me that he was taking her out to dinner because she was depressed. It makes more sense that she killed herself. He wouldn't do something like that."

"You just don't want to believe anything bad about that man because you're falling for him."

"No. It's because that man is a *good* man."

I thought about what Mason must be going through. He'd tried helping her and probably felt responsible for not being able to save her. That was also the kind of man he was.

"I think I should fly out to New York today. He needs my support," I said, thinking out loud.

She gasped. "What?"

"He's not guilty of anything but trying to help her. She obviously needed the professional kind."

"Terrabae..."

"Celine. I know what I'm talking about," I said sharply. "You don't know him the way that I do."

She sighed. "Fine. If you do fly out there, call me and let me know what you find out. Just... be careful. I know you trust Mason, but you're thinking with your heart right now, not your mind."

I sighed. "I'll call you when I learn more," I said and hung up.

Three hours had passed, and there was still no word from Mason. Anxious and worried about him, I called the airlines and changed my flight to one for two-o'clock today. Then I quickly put the finishing touches on the cake, asked Marcella to get it ready for delivery, and raced home to pack.

Chapter 33

Mason

The cops spent hours questioning me about Zondra's death. In the beginning I told them I didn't need a lawyer, but I eventually regretted it. Especially since they kept trying to pin her death on me, which was totally insane.

"This is a waste of time. I didn't have anything to do with it!" I snapped, feeling not only angry, but... devastated. I blew out a breath and raked my hand through my hair. "We were friends. *Good* friends, which is why we went out last night in the first place. She was depressed about her ex."

"Zed and Palmer claimed that you were the last to see her. Did you go up to her room?" asked Detective Johnson, ignoring me.

"Yes. I walked her to her suite, but I didn't go inside."

He smirked. "Why not? We heard you two used to be a 'thing'. Maybe a little TLC would have put a smile on her face and made things less depressing."

"Sex doesn't solve everything, and our 'thing' was a long time ago," I replied angrily.

"Do you know why they were getting divorced?" asked Detective Pohl, the other cop.

"She said he didn't love her anymore. That's all I know," I replied, exhausted from answering the same questions.

"We've been told you usually have security guards around twenty-four seven," said Johnson. "Where were they this morning?"

"I dismissed them. I told Mack I didn't want them around constantly," I said. "Do you know what it's like being shadowed day-and-night? It gets really old."

"Not all rock stars have bodyguards tailing them constantly. Why did you?" Johnson asked.

I told him about Stalker John and his threats. "Ask my manager about it. Hell, someone just tried breaking into my place in Beverly Hills. Look that up."

"Mack Calhoun? We've talked to him already. He didn't mention anything about a stalker," said Pohl.

"That's probably because it's unrelated to this and he didn't think about it at the time you were questioning him," I said.

"You mentioned that you lost your phone earlier. When did that happen?" Johnson asked, writing things down.

"I'm not exactly sure. I had it at the restaurant and then when we met up with Zed and Palmer, I couldn't find it," I replied wearily.

"Where do you usually keep it on your person? Do you have a clip?" he asked.

"I usually keep it in one of my jacket pockets," I said, shoving my hands inside and pulling out the empty liners.

"Do you think you might have dropped it?" Pohl asked.

"Maybe. We took a cab to Apotheke and it's possible it fell out there. Or in the cab. I don't know, maybe it was even stolen," I replied, trying to remember when I'd last even noticed it in my pocket.

The questions went on until there was nothing else left to answer. Since they had no evidence on me, they eventually let me go.

"If you can think of anything else that might help with this case, call me," Detective Johnson said, handing me his card.

"Sure." I shoved it into my wallet. "Was there a note left behind or anything?"

"A suicide note? No," Detective Pohl said. "Nothing."

I thought it was a little strange. The Zondra I knew would have left a letter. She would have wanted to say goodbye or maybe given some kind of explanation. Of course, I also had no idea that she'd leap off of her balcony, either. I didn't know what to think anymore.

Mack was waiting for me when I walked out of the interrogation room. He looked agitated.

"Why didn't you call your lawyer?" he asked me.

"Because, I'm not guilty of anything," I said as we headed toward the front doors of the precinct.

"Doesn't matter. He could have gotten you out of here hours ago."

"I know. I guess I made a mistake," I replied, rubbing the stubble on my face. "Just like last night."

"What's that supposed to mean?" he asked.

"I should have never left Zondra. She was obviously more distraught than I could have ever imagined."

"You didn't know she was going to do a swan-dive off of her balcony," Mack replied. "Don't blame yourself."

But, I did. She'd asked me to spend the night and if I

would have, the woman would still be alive. I shouldn't have felt guilty, but I damn well did. For once, I'd done the right thing, but it had cost Zondra her life.

WHEN I ARRIVED back at my hotel room, I searched the Internet and found the phone number for *Sweet Treats* and called it. Unfortunately, she wasn't around.

"Do you have her cell phone number?" I asked.

"I can't give that out. Wait a second, is this Mason Stone?" the gal asked.

"Yeah."

"Oh, hi! It's me. Cindy."

"Hi, Cindy. I really need to get in touch with Terra."

"Is it true about that woman, Zondra? Did she kill herself?" Cindy asked.

So, they already knew about it. "We think so."

"I saw on the news that you were the last person to see her."

I had to keep from losing my cool and reminded myself that she was just young and star-struck.

"I can't talk about it. But, I'd like to talk to Terra. Can you please give me her number?" I asked a little more sharply then I'd intended to.

"I'm sorry, Mason. I've been instructed to never give her home or cell phone number out."

It was then that I remembered I still had Terra's business card somewhere in my suitcase.

Idiot, I thought. *I'd had her number all along!*

"I've gotta go," I said and hung up.

After searching through my luggage, I found the card and immediately called her cell phone. She didn't answer, so I left a voicemail begging her to call me. I also gave her the name of the hotel I was staying at and my room number.

"I lost my cell phone last night and I'm sure you've heard the news about Zondra. I was called in for questioning and that's where I was most of the day," I explained. "Please, call me as soon as you can. I need to hear your voice."

Chapter 34

Terra

By the time we made it to New York, it was almost seven p.m. and the JFK International Airport was crazy busy.

Let the fun begin, I thought wryly.

Pulling the cell phone out of my purse, I took it out of airplane mode and immediately noticed I'd missed a call and a voicemail from a number I didn't recognize. When I heard Mason's voice, I smiled in relief.

After listening to his message, I tried calling his hotel room, but couldn't reach him. In turn, I left a voicemail, telling him where I was and then went in search of my luggage.

By the time I found my suitcase and stepped out of the building, my anxiety level was almost through the roof. Fortunately, I found a cab right away and gave the driver the name of Mason's hotel.

"You okay, miss?" the cabbie asked, looking at me with concern.

"I'm fine. Thank you. I just hate airports," I replied.

He grinned. "Ah. I'll get you out of here quickly then. Personally, I don't like 'em either. But, they help pay my bills, you know what I mean?"

"Oh, totally. And, thank you," I said, relaxing as we pulled away from the curb.

"Anytime.'

Forty-five minutes later I was in the Plaza Hotel's elevator and on my way to Mason's suite, relieved and excited to see him. Taking out my phone, I tried calling him once again, but there was still no answer.

"He's probably having dinner," I told myself as the elevator dinged and opened. "Or, with Mack."

Grabbing the handle of my suitcase, I rolled it down the hallway and began searching for Mason's room number. When I finally found it, I knocked, but there was no answer. Sighing, I walked back to the elevator and sat down on one of the wing-back chairs. I knew there was no use roaming the hotel and that the staff wouldn't let me into his room. I would wait as long as it took for Mason to return, or someone else I recognized from his band.

I stayed there for what seemed like forever, waiting and watching as people came and went. One man in particular, a nice looking guy who seemed friendly enough, passed me by a few times and then eventually asked if I needed help. I thought it was a very nice gesture, especially since he looked like a guest and not a hotel employee.

"I'm fine. I'm just waiting for someone," I replied, smiling. "Thank you, though."

"No problem." He studied my face for a minute. "You look familiar. Wait a second, are you waiting for Mason Stone?"

I sat up straighter. "Yes, I am. Do you know where he is?"

The man grinned. "He's back in my hotel room. I'll take you there."

"Oh. Okay. Who are you?" I asked, standing up.

"I'm with the security team. After the incident last night, we decided he'd be safer staying in a different room."

"Really? Is he in danger?" I asked, confused.

"We're not sure, which is why he's been moved. Come on, I'll take you to him."

As I was following the stranger down the hallway, I stared at the back of his camp shirt. It was black and had yellow flowers on it. Very touristy and nothing like the clothing the security guards had worn in Minneapolis. Most of them had worn suits and ties.

"Are you hungry?" he asked, looking back at me over his shoulder. "I've ordered a pizza for Mason and it should be arriving soon."

"Yeah, actually, I'm pretty hungry," I replied.

"That's what I thought. We'll have ourselves a little party."

A party?

"Here we are," he said, pulling out his hotel key card. He opened the door and turned to me. "I can take your luggage."

"No, it's okay. I've got it," I replied, feeling suddenly strange about the situation. It just didn't feel right.

The man moved out of my way and motioned for me to step inside. "Mason," he called out, an eerie smile on his face. "You have a visitor."

Staring at him, I waited for Mason to answer, but he didn't.

"Mason?" I said loudly, the hair standing up on the back of my neck. Something wasn't right.

When he didn't answer, I took a step back. "You know, I think I'll just wait back by the elevators for him. He must have stepped out or something."

202

The man's smile turned into a scowl. Before I could react, he grabbed my arm roughly and pulled me into the room.

Terrified, I tried screaming, but he covered my mouth with his palm and then shoved a gun up to my temple.

"You make any loud sounds, and I'll blow your head off," he growled, glaring at me.

Frightened out of my mind, all I could do was nod.

Chapter 35

Mason

Mack bought me and the rest of the band dinner at the restaurant in our hotel. It was a somber meal and all we talked about was Zondra and what a tragic loss it had been.

"She was having fun last night, too," Zed said, looking stricken. "I just don't get it."

"Me neither," Palmer said, also looking distraught. "It all seems so surreal."

I felt sick to my stomach. I desperately wanted to go back in time and talk to her. Not sleep with her, but just talk...

"So, are we still doing the concert Friday night?" Zed asked sadly. "It wouldn't be the same without her opening up for us."

"No," replied Mack. "It's been canceled."

He sighed in relief. "Good."

Mack stirred his rum and Coke and took a sip. "We're going to need to find another opening band, obviously."

"Or maybe we can just cancel the rest of the tour," I suggested. "People would understand."

"We might have to if they don't rule her death as a suicide," Zed said.

"It *was* suicide," I said sharply. "Nobody killed her. Certainly not me."

"I didn't say you did. Sheesh," he said, frowning. "I'm

just saying that this thing could haunt us for a long time. Especially if they're trying to pin something on you."

Closing my eyes, I ran a hand over my face. "They have nothing on me. Plus, I'm innocent."

"Of course you are," Mack said, an edge to his voice. "But, you should still contact your lawyer, though. You *need* legal protection. Innocent people go to jail, too, you know."

I let out a ragged sigh. "Yeah. Maybe I would. If I had a *phone.*"

"You should be getting your new one soon. I called this morning and ordered you a new one," Mack said.

"Thanks," I replied.

He nodded. "You bet."

"I still have no idea where I lost it," I replied, running a hand through my hair. "It's driving me crazy."

"Probably someone picked your pocket," Mack said. "There's a lot of that here. Busy city."

I nodded and pushed my chair back. "I'm tired. I'm heading upstairs." I also wanted to check my hotel room phone messages.

"Get some sleep. You deserve it," Mack said.

"Thanks," I replied and then said goodbye to the others.

When I arrived at my suite, I found that I indeed had messages. Three of them. Two were from Terra. The third was from a stranger. As I listened, my blood turned to ice.

"Mason Stone... I have something of yours," the unknown caller said, a smile in his voice. "If you want to see her alive again, you'd better do exactly what I say."

The next thing I heard was Terra, crying and saying my name. Hearing the terror in her voice, I had to sit down before my legs buckled underneath me.

"You recognize her don't you?" the man said and laughed darkly. "I do. From your cell phone, which I'm sure you're missing very much right now. Nice set of tits, by the way. I wonder how she'd look without them?"

I gasped in horror.

"Wait for my next call," he said. "And keep the police out of it or you'll never see Terra again."

That was the end of the message.

"Fuck!" I yelled. I picked up the closest thing within my reach, which was the bedside lamp, and yanked its cord from the wall before throwing it across the room. I then slumped down against the edge of the bed and fell to the floor and put my face in my hands.

Chapter 36
Terra

I stared at the man who I'd learned was named Byron Phillips. Apparently, he'd been married to Zondra and she'd broken his heart.

"Your little man-whore thinks he can have everyone he wants. But not anymore. Not Zondra and not you."

I stared at him with tears in my eyes. I wanted to tell Byron that there'd been nothing going on between Zondra and Mason, but he'd put duct tape over my mouth. My ankles and wrists were also bound by it. I was trapped with a mad man.

"I saw them together last night," he said, pacing back and forth in the hotel room. He bit the side of his nail and smiled coldly. "Eating dinner and laughing and flirting with each other. She lied to me. She said there wasn't anything between them. But, I saw it. I *always* saw it."

From his words, I gathered that Byron was the man who'd been stalking Mason and sending him death threats. The infamous Stalker John. Now he was talking about killing him, like he'd apparently killed Zondra a few hours before.

"It's almost time," he said, looking at his watch. "Let's just hope he doesn't try anything stupid. You'd also better hope, for your sake, that he doesn't bring in the cops or this entire floor is going to go up in smoke."

My eyes widened.

Grinning maniacally, Byron opened up his suitcase. Inside was something I was pretty sure was a bomb of some kind.

"You know what that is, don't you?" he asked, walking over to me. He reached up and began stroking my hair. "Sure you do."

Glaring at him, I pulled away.

"You'd better be nice or I'll make good on my threats," he said, groping at my chest.

I narrowed my eyes at him and growled at him under the duct tape.

Byron chuckled, and then his face went murderous. He reared his hand back and slapped me clean across the face.

My eyes filled with tears and I put my head down and sobbed.

Mason

The kidnapper called me back at exactly nine o'clock. He instructed me to leave my hotel room, go to the elevators, and take them down to the mezzanine. From there, I was supposed to wait for further instruction.

"I want to talk to Terra," I said before we hung up. I was shaking with rage. "I'm not doing anything until I do."

"Fine."

A few seconds later, Terra was on the phone.

"Mason, don't meet him. Call the—"

There was a loud slap and then the guy got back on the

phone.

"Don't listen to her. She's going to get you *both* killed," he warned.

"You touch her again and I'll fucking kill you," I growled.

He grunted. "Listen carefully, leave in exactly three minutes. Don't be late. Don't bring any weapons. But do... come alone."

The kidnapper hung up.

Frustrated and terrified, I opened up my suitcase and searched around for something I could use against the asshole. I didn't have a gun or a sharp knife. I vowed to change that in the future. Noticing my replacement razor blades, I grabbed one. It seemed like a long shot, but it was small and could definitely do a lot of damage. Plus, it was all I had.

Glancing at the clock, I saw with annoyance that my time was running out. I quickly walked out of the suite and waved off my security when they tried to follow me. They were already suspicious because they'd flown into the room after I broke the lamp, but I had told them it was nothing and they had reluctantly agreed to stay posted up outside my room.

I headed to the elevators, and when I arrived, there was another man standing there and waiting.

He turned and looked at me. "Hey," he said. "Remember me?"

Blinking, I suddenly recognized the guy. It was Zondra's ex-husband. "Byron, what are..." my tongue froze as I realized why he was there and smiling like a crazy lunatic.

"Come with me," he said, pulling out a gun. "Now."

Chapter 37

Terra

Once Byron left, I tried struggling against the duct tape, but was given little time because Byron returned momentarily. This time, with Mason.

I was both relieved and terrified to see Mason had come alone.

"Oh, isn't this special?" Byron said sarcastically, as Mason rushed over to where I was tied to the desk chair and put his arms around me protectively. "Two lovers unite. All is right with the world now, isn't it?" He smile disappeared. "*Not.*"

Mason glared at him as he put himself in front of me protectively. "What in the hell is wrong with you, Byron?"

"This is what happens to a man when everything he has is taken from him," Byron replied with a bitter smile.

"Cut the bullshit," Mason said. He sat next to me on the bed, and with one hand he reached back to where my hands were tied. I could feel him secretly trying to cut the tape with something as he kept his eyes on my abductor. "Why are you doing this?"

"*You* made me do it. You," he growled, glaring at him. "It wasn't enough that you're this bigshot celebrity, but you had to take the one thing that meant something to me. Zondra."

"I didn't take anyone from you!" Mason said angrily.

"The lies just never stop," he said, staring at him with murder in his eyes.

Mason's eyes blazed angrily. "Listen, man, whatever you

think happened between Zondra and me... it didn't."

"You're only saying that because your lady-friend is here, but we both know the truth. You and Zondra were having an affair," he replied.

"That's bullshit. Zondra and I dated a long, *long* time ago. Before she ever met you. It didn't work out though because there wasn't enough chemistry. Why would we pick back up on something that wasn't ever there?"

"Liar," he said, clenching his teeth. "You were with her last night."

"I took Zondra to dinner because she was depressed and needed someone to talk to about the man who broke her fucking heart. A man who was still on her mind when she killed herself. Unless..." Mason paused and his eyes grew wide. "She *didn't* kill herself?"

Byron's hand began to shake but he said nothing.

"You killed her, didn't you?" he said angrily, just as my wrists broke free from the tape.

"She killed herself. Long ago when she cheated on me with you."

Mason growled in frustration. "We *weren't* having an affair. Your twisted mind made it all up. It was you who ruined your marriage. You're the one who broke her heart when all she did was try and prove her love to you."

Byron's face looked like it was about to shatter. "That's not true!" His eyes filled with tears. "You're lying. You're just trying to make me feel guilty."

"Too bad you killed her. She'd tell you all of this herself," Mason said, putting something small and sharp in my hand. Realizing it was a razor, I clutched it firmly in my palm.

Byron stood there frozen and crying.

"Dammit, let us go," Mason said. "You made a mistake, but you still have time to correct it."

His lips curled into a scowl. He wagged his finger. "You... you *almost* had me. But I'm not as gullible as you think. You'll say anything to stay alive."

"You want money? Let Terra go and I'll give you whatever you need to flee the country and start over," Mason said.

"I don't want your money," he snapped. "What I want is for you to back away from her and over to the other chair."

Mason didn't move.

"Now!" ordered Byron waving the gun at him.

Raising his hands in surrender, Mason did as he was told. "Just take it easy."

Keeping the gun trained on Mason, Byron moved over to the dresser and grabbed the roll of duct tape. "Sit down."

Mason sat.

Byron moved behind Mason. "Put your wrists together."

"No," he said.

"You want me to shoot your girlfriend right fucking now? I will," Byron replied, now aiming the gun at me.

"God, no!" Mason's panicked expression startled me. "Look, someone will hear the gunshot, Byron. They'll call the cops and you'll never get away."

"The gun has a silencer. Now, put your wrists together or I shoot the bitch."

Mason put his hands behind the chair and Byron began taping his wrists together. I stared at Mason, feeling helpless. Although my wrists were free, my ankles were not. I'd fall flat on my face before I could try and get away.

"There," said Byron, standing up. He walked around to the front of the chair and Mason tried kicking him.

"Looks like it's ankles tied, too," Byron snarled. "Stop moving or I'll shoot you in the thigh. Better yet, I'll shoot you in the crotch and enjoy watching you bleed to death."

Mason moved his feet together and looked at me.

Byron kneeled down in front of him with the tape.

"Now," Mason mouthed, nodding toward my ankles.

I quickly leaned down with the razor blade and began sawing at the duct tape. Fortunately, Byron was too busy wrapping Mason's ankles to notice and suddenly... I was free.

Watching me, Mason nodded toward the doorway, but I knew that running away and actually getting away would be a long shot. Especially when the man had a gun. Instead, I picked up my suitcase, crept behind Byron, and hit him on top of the head as hard as I could. Gasping in pain, he fell over, but didn't pass out like they always did in the movies.

Shit!

Moaning, Byron began to get back up.

"Run!" ordered Mason.

I knew that if I got away, he would shoot Mason and leave before the cops came. I wasn't about to abandon him.

I could never live with myself. Thinking back to the wrestling matches I used to watch with my dad as a child, I jumped onto Byron's back and put him in a choke-hold.

Releasing the gun, Byron tried pulling my arm away from

his neck and eventually succeeded. Suddenly, he was on top of me and had his hands on my throat.

"Let her go!" Mason cried out, struggling to get out of the chair.

Gasping for breath, my first reaction was to dig my fingernails into Byron's hands, but it did nothing. Then I remembered the razorblade. I saw it lying on the floor a few inches away, as I must have dropped it when I picked up the suitcase. My fingers were barely able to reach it. I slid it over to me and without a second thought, reached up and slashed him across the face with it.

"You bitch!" Byron hollered, rearing his head back.

I did it again, this time across his eyebrow, drawing a lot more blood.

Swearing some more, Byron released me and tried going for the gun, but I kicked it away and desperately reached for him again. I couldn't let him get his hands on that pistol.

Chapter 38

Mason

I felt helpless watching them struggle. I couldn't move because of the duct tape, and was frustrated that she hadn't tried to escape.

After Terra cut Byron with the razorblade the second time, he went for the gun. Fortunately, she was able to kick it away and then somehow pin him down.

I was *damn* proud of her.

But, I also knew she was in trouble. Byron was wiry, but he was stronger than her and it was only a matter of time before he regained the upper hand.

I had to do something.

Using all my weight, I toppled the chair over, causing a loud distraction. It worked because Byron froze and looked over to see what I was doing.

Taking advantage of this, Terra did something I couldn't see that caused him to scream in agony. She then crawled off of him and went for the gun. The next thing I knew, she was on her back and aiming the weapon at Byron, who was moaning and cupping his balls.

I sighed in relief. *She must have hurt the bastard where the sun don't shine…*

Realizing he was no longer a serious threat, Terra stood up and rushed over to me. "Are you okay?"

"Yes. Don't worry about me, though. Keep the gun trained on him and call the police."

"Okay."

Suddenly there was a sharp rap on the door.

"This is hotel security. Is everything all right in there?" someone called out.

"Oh, thank God," Terra said and raced to open the door. As she did this, I watched Byron struggle to his feet. His face was now covered in so much of his own blood, it was a grisly sight.

"Freeze and put the gun down!" I heard a stern voice snap.

Realizing she'd answered the door with the gun still in her hand, my heart felt like it was going to implode. I waited for the sound of gunfire from security and sighed in relief when it never came.

"Oh, my God, I'm sorry," she replied in a shaky voice and tossed the pistol to the floor, where the security guard kicked it out of her reach.

Meanwhile, Byron limped over to the sliding glass door and opened it as hotel security entered the room.

"You there, stay where you are!" one of them ordered.

Ignoring them, Byron stepped outside.

"Does he have a gun?" one of them asked, a tall, hard-faced bald guy.

"Not anymore," Terra replied, indicating the gun on the floor.

He rushed out onto the balcony and I heard him swear.

"What is it?" asked one of the other officers.

"We got another jumper," he replied, turning around with a grimace.

Chapter 39

Terra

Three Months Later

I looked at Mason. "Are you ready?" We'd just pulled up to RJ's Diner to meet his father.

He blew out a breath and nodded.

Sally, the waitress, had called twenty minutes ago, and just by chance, Mason was back in town. He'd just sold his mansion in California and was now living in my condo temporarily.

We got out of my Enclave and went into the diner. It was lunchtime, so the place was packed and there were people waiting to be seated.

Seeing us, Sally walked over carrying a coffeepot.

"Where is he?" Mason murmured.

She smiled and pointed. "He's in the end-booth over there."

We looked over. The two people seated there looked like a nice, ordinary couple having a pleasant meal while enjoying each other's company. I didn't know what I'd expected, but the man who was supposed to be Mason's father didn't seem to resemble Mason, as far as I could tell.

"Is that him?" I asked, wondering if Sally had made a mistake.

"I'm not sure," Mason replied, staring in that direction.

"It's him," Sally said. "You'll see when you get close."

"Does he know I'm coming?" Mason asked, turning to her.

"I don't know for sure. I talked to his wife, Emily, and told her you were coming, though."

We'd learned from Sally that Mason's father had been in an accident a few years earlier, caused by his drinking. The only person hurt in the accident had been him. From what Sally had found out, Len had sustained a head injury. There'd been a significant amount of memory loss and he was still having issues with remembering his past. His new wife, Emily, he'd met through AA, and both of them were recovering alcoholics. Fortunately, through it all, they'd found love and happiness together.

"Does he even know he has a son?" Mason asked.

"You're going to have to find that out for yourself," Sally said, looking at the couple.

Mason sighed.

I grabbed his hand and squeezed.

He looked at me. "Thank you for coming with me."

"I'd do anything for you. You know that," I replied softly.

"I love you," he said, leaning down and kissing me.

We'd been saying it ever since the Byron incident. Mason had told me first, claiming he knew the moment he thought he was going to lose me that he was in love with me. I was pretty sure I knew I was in love with him when I'd learned about Zondra's death. All I cared about at the time was getting to the man I loved so he wouldn't have to face everything alone.

"I love you, too," I replied.

Holding hands, we walked over to the booth where Len

and Emily were seated, drinking coffee.

Mason's father looked up and it immediately gave me goosebumps.

"Hello there," Emily said, smiling. "You must be Mason?"

Staring at his father, who looked very confused, Mason nodded.

"Mason?" Len said, a faraway look in his eyes. He scratched his chin. "Hmm…"

Mason's eyes filled with tears. "Hi, Dad."

Len's eyes opened wide. "Dad?"

He nodded. "Don't… don't you remember me?" he asked in a husky voice.

Len looked at Emily. She touched his hand and smiled.

"Mason." His face suddenly became animated as he looked at his son. "Your mother used to sing lullabies to you," he said. His lips trembled and he smiled sadly. "She had a beautiful voice."

Mason nodded and looked away for a second, quickly swiping at a tear from his cheek.

Len slid out of the booth and stood up next to him. They were almost the same height.

He pointed at Mason. "Yes, I remember now," he said, staring at him in wonder. "You're my son. Mason."

Mason nodded.

Len looked him up and down. "You've grown. When did that happen?"

Mason laughed. "A while ago."

"You were always so talented. I remember those plays

you did and that voice. You didn't get that from me," he said.

Mason grinned. "From mom."

"Yes." He put his hand on Mason's shoulder and squeezed. "You got it from your mother. She was always so proud of you. I was, too... even though... I had a hard time showing it," Len's eyes filled with tears. He wrapped his arms around Mason and hugged him. "I'm so sorry... So... sorry..."

"It's okay, Dad," Mason said, quietly, fighting back emotion.

My own eyes filled with tears watching the exchange. I looked at Emily to see she had the same reaction.

"No. It's not. I did you wrong. I..." Len pulled away and stared at Mason. "You were my son and I treated you badly. I don't deserve your forgiveness."

"I'm still your son and everyone deserves forgiveness. Especially, you," he said in a ragged voice.

Len stood there for a few seconds and then nodded. "I never said this enough. Especially after your mother died. I was selfish and destructive. Not anymore. No more wasted time. I *love* you, Son."

"I love you, too, Pop," he replied softly.

Everyone in the diner began to clap and it was then that I realized how quiet it had become.

"This is my son, everyone! His name is Mason," Len said, patting him on his back with a look of pride.

"We know who he is," a woman called out, chuckling.

"She knows you? Do you eat here a lot?" Len asked, looking confused again.

"We can talk about it later," Mason answered, laughing softly.

Len looked down at the table again. "Emily, dear, meet my son."

Emily raised her hand and Mason shook it. "Nice to meet you," she said, her eyes sparkling.

"A pleasure meeting you, too," he replied.

"And who is this pretty young woman?" Len asked, now smiling at me.

Mason pulled me closer. "This is my future wife. I hope," he said smiling down at me.

I stared at him in shock. "What?"

Mason smiled. "I was going to wait and do this," he pulled a small, black box out of his leather jacket, "but, this seems to be my lucky day and I'm hoping it stays that way." He took a deep breath and got down on his knee. "Terra. Sweet Cakes…"

I blushed, hearing some of the customers laugh at the endearment.

"I love you with all of my heart. Not only do you support and inspire me, but you've given me the courage to let go of the things holding me back from my true dreams, which include you. Us. A family. I can't imagine living without you and I hope you feel the same way. Will you marry me?" he asked, opening up the velvet box.

"Yes," I squealed before even looking at the ring. I didn't care if it was the tab from of a can of soda or the most expensive rock on the planet. I loved Mason with all of my heart and I couldn't imagine a life without him either. "I'll marry you."

When he stood, the patrons began clapping and whooping. I looked around to see we were given a standing ovation, most of them with happy expressions, some with tears in their eyes, and some people with their phones out, filming us with huge smiles on their faces.

Mason shook his head at them with a smile, and then kissed me like he'd never kissed me before.

"You've made me the happiest man in the world," he breathed. "I don't think anything could top this feeling I have right now."

Epilogue
Mason
Two Years Later

"It's a boy!" the doctor said, grinning. "A healthy one at that."

My heart felt like it was overflowing as I stared at my crying son for the very first time. The love and pure joy I felt was overwhelming; it brought tears to my eyes. I leaned down and kissed my exhausted, beautiful wife, Terra, who'd been in labor for almost two days. After hours of endless contractions, they'd finally given her a C-section when the baby's heartrate had started to drop.

"I want to see," Terra pouted, unable to get a good view from her position.

"Just one second, mom. Mason, do you want to cut the cord?" the doctor asked.

Shaking, I stepped over and tried to avoid looking at all the blood and goo as he showed me what to do. When I'd finished, a nurse brought our son over to Terra.

"He's beautiful," Terra said, crying tears of joy and kissing him on his reddish purple head. He was still whimpering.

"They'll clean him up, weigh, and measure him," said the doctor. "We gotta stitch you back up now, Mrs. Stone. Then you can hold your baby. What's his name?"

"Brandon Leonard Stone," I said.

Brandon had been Terra's father's name and we'd wanted to honor his memory by naming our first child after him.

Leonard, of course, for my father.

"Nice name," the doctor said. "Would you like to give Brandon his first bath, Mason?"

"Sure," I said, both anxious and nervous. The baby looked so small and delicate. It was crazy to realize that we'd walked into the hospital as a couple, and were now a family of three.

"Follow the nurse," the doctor said with a knowing smile.

Trembling from the rush of emotions I was feeling, I quickly kissed my wife and the followed the quick-footed nurse who was holding my son. The lyrics to a new song began forming in my head.

Terra

When they finally handed me my baby, I was back in my room, sore, but excited to see Brandon. When he looked up at me with Mason's big, blue eyes, and our gazes met for the first time, I knew I would never be the same. The love I felt for my child was like nothing I could have ever imagined.

"He's perfect, too," Mason said, leaning down. "I gave him his first bath. Strapping young lad, I must say."

I snorted. "Okay, so you're saying he looks a lot like you?"

"Yep," he said, taking a sip of soda. "A chip off the old block. That's my boy."

Mason wasn't kidding. He looked like he was going to have a lot of his same features which, as a mother, I knew would be both a blessing and a curse.

"The girls will go crazy for you one day," I whispered, kissing Brandon's forehead. "And probably some of the boys."

Mason grunted.

"You never know. He could be gay. Look at my mother," I replied. "Anyway, it doesn't matter what his sexual preference ends up being, we'll love him regardless."

"I don't think we should concern ourselves with his sex life just yet. I can't believe you're even thinking that far ahead."

"You're the one who was boasting about..."

"Enough," Mason said with a pained look. "It's a father thing. We want our sons to be perfect. Let's just keep it at that."

I laughed. Picking on him was so much fun.

"Hello?" called a voice from the door. "Anyone home?"

"Speaking of which," Mason said, turning around. "Hello, Grandma Maria."

"Hello," she said, walking in with balloons and a small teddy bear wearing a pale blue bow-tie. "How's my new grandson doing?"

"Here. You can hold him and find out," I said, smiling.

"Where's Jackie?" asked Mason.

Mom handed him the balloons and set the bear down. "She's at *Sweet Treats* finishing up a wedding cake. She said she'll stop by before dinner."

Jackie and my mother were both helping out with the business now. Jackie had even taken several classes on cake

225

decorating and was surprisingly very creative. I'd also taught her a few tricks, and now many of her cakes even outshined mine. It was good knowing that the bakery was in such good hands now.

"Okay," I said.

"Look at you. You're so precious," my mother gushed as she took Brandon from me and kissed his little nose.

"By the way, Celine just texted you. She's stopping in with the twins," Mason said, reading my cell phone.

I groaned. As much as I loved my best friend, her twins were a handful. The boys had just learned to walk and were always into everything. I knew because I'd been watching them quite a bit, trying to get a taste of motherhood.

"Don't worry. I'll be here to corral them if things get too crazy," Mason said, smiling. He knew.

"What about your father?" I asked him.

"Emily is bringing him tomorrow. He wanted to make sure you had enough rest after the surgery," he replied.

Len was a really sweet man. I could see what Mason's mother and Emily had seen in him. Fortunately, he was doing very well with his memory care therapy, and his memory had mostly returned. He and Mason were closer than ever. They spent every Sunday afternoon together, either fishing, golfing, or watching football together, depending on the season.

"That's very considerate of him," I said, moving slowly. The C-section had been a frightening concept, but it had gone much more smoothly than I'd anticipated. Especially after they gave me something for the pain, which had been almost unbearable during labor.

"So, how's business, Mason?" my mother asked.

226

After we got married, Mason split away from *My Life In Chaos* and now owned a jazz club in Minneapolis, called *Chaotic Blues*. Although he featured different bands, sometimes Mason would play some of his own music, which usually drew in a large crowd. But, jazz was the main focus of the club and so it didn't happen very often.

"It's going well," he replied. "Thank you for asking, Mother Maria."

I snorted at his nickname for her. He thought it made her sound like a nun, which my mother was far from being.

"So, you don't miss being center stage?" she asked, eyeing him curiously.

"Not really," said Mason. "Don't get me wrong; when I do get nostalgic, I have to play something, and since it's my club, the customers are forced to listen."

My mother and I laughed.

"Forced to listen," I snorted. "Right."

He went on. "Honestly, though, I love the way things are. I can be home with my family when I want and not have to travel from city-to-city for months on end."

"You don't miss being in the limelight at all?" she asked.

"I'm just in a different kind of limelight," he replied, staring down at Brandon. "I'm a father now. I don't want to mess that up. I've seen it happen to celebrities who put their careers first."

My mother smiled at me. "Okay, he's a keeper."

"I know, right?" I said, grabbing his hand and squeezing it.

Mason leaned down and kissed me. "You're the keeper. I still can't believe how close I came to losing you back in

New York. I still have nightmares about that."

"Really?" I said, staring up at him with a sad smile.

He nodded. "But, it also brought us to where we are today."

"Our lives were never meant to be easy," my mother said. "We each have our own obstacle courses to overcome. From the moment we take our first breath, our journey begins."

"I'm sorry, did someone just turn on the Learning Channel?" I said, chuckling. "I swear I hear a documentary running somewhere."

She smiled. "Ha-ha," Mom said dryly. "I'm just giving you some motherly advice which is... to hold him close but don't smother him."

I understood exactly what she was talking about. I used the same philosophy with Mason and it worked. Our relationship was happy and healthy. I trusted him and he trusted me.

"I hear you, Mom," I said, closing my eyes and opening them. I was weak and sore. The nurse was going to be coming for me soon. Apparently, I was supposed to get up and walk, which sounded scary, considering the surgery I'd just had.

"You're probably exhausted. By the way, I can't stay long, but I'll be back in tomorrow," she said, walking around the room with Brandon and rocking him gently.

"No problem," I said.

"Get some sleep while you can. You won't get any once you bring him home," she said.

"So, I've heard," I replied.

We talked about when I was a baby and how my father
228

and she used to take turns getting up with me.

"Of course, I had to use formula," she said. "I couldn't breastfeed. Are you going to?"

I nodded. "I'm going to give it my best shot."

"Just don't drown the kid," Mason joked. "We might need to buy him goggles for when he's feeding from those sprinklers."

"Not funny," I said dryly.

"You have no idea what it's like to be top-heavy," my mother said, although she was laughing. "The horrible back pain. I had mine reduced and have never regretted it for a second."

Mason looked at me. "Do they really bring you a lot of pain?"

"Sometimes," I admitted with a nod. "I mean, now they really do because I just had a baby and am producing milk."

"Maybe you should think about having them reduced, too, then," he said, surprising me. "I don't want you to be uncomfortable."

"We'll see how things go in the months ahead," I replied, grateful that I wasn't with someone who cared more about the size of my breasts than my daily comfort.

"Whatever you want. I just want you to be happy," he said.

"Is he always this nice, or is it because I'm here?" my mother asked.

"It's definitely because you're here," Mason said with a smile. "When you're away, I become a complete asshole."

I rolled my eyes and teased, "Language—in front of your

son."

He shot me a look, and went on. "I'm kidding. I'm actually very nice and for good reason. I've seen her with a razor blade. She's... unstoppable. I would have hired her for my security team if I would have known what a badass you raised, Mother Maria."

She laughed. "Oh, God, how do you put up with him?"

"We all have our obstacles to overcome," I said, repeating her in a dramatic voice.

"Oh, you two." Mom looked down at Brandon. "Your parents are quite the characters. Good luck, kiddo. Just remember, you can come and stay with Grandma whenever you want."

Mason and I smiled at each other.

WHEN MY MOTHER finally left, Mason scratched his head and smiled.

"What is it?" I asked.

"I see a lot of your mother in you," he replied.

"Oh?"

"It's a compliment," he said. "She's an amazing woman."

"Yes. She is, isn't she?" I said with a wistful smile.

"I hope our next one is a girl."

My smile fell. "You're *already* thinking of more kids? I hate to break it to you... but this was no picnic in the park. It actually hurt like a son-of-a-bitch."

He looked disappointed. "So, you don't want any more?"

"Let's just enjoy Brandon for a while first, okay?"

"Yeah. Of course."

"And no pouting. We have a child now. I don't need two pouty boys to deal with. One will be bad enough."

"Someone's got to teach him the proper way to pout," Mason said.

Brandon started to get fussy and Mason took him from me. "Let me show you how it's done," he said.

Amused, I watched Mason attempt to soothe Brandon, who I figured was probably getting hungry. When rocking didn't help, he began to sing him a lullaby in that amazing voice of his. Immediately, the baby stopped crying, and it was now me who was crying at how beautiful it was seeing my husband sing to our son.

Damn hormones.

"My mother used to sing that one to me," Mason said softly afterward, staring down at Brandon with so much love, it made my heart swell.

I knew right then and there that if he wanted more children, I would gladly give them to him. He'd had such a tough childhood, and something told me it was one reason why fatherhood meant so much to him now.

"Okay."

He looked at me. "Okay?"

"We can have more children."

He grinned. "Soon?"

"I'm pretty sure I'll have to wait a year to fully recover from the surgery. After the doctor gives us the green light to try again. Okay?"

"Definitely. How does that sound Brandon, my boy?

Would you like a little baby brother or sister?"

In response, Brandon scrunched up his face and took his first major poop.

"I guess he wants to wait," Mason said, holding the baby out toward me. "Here."

"Don't look at me, I just had surgery. You're going to have to be the one to change him." I knew I could probably handle it, as I'd changed a couple of the twins' dirty diapers when Celine had had her hands full. But Mason needed to jump into it right away. I had a feeling that I'd always be the one changing him if I didn't put my foot down now.

His eyes filled with panic. "But, I've never changed a diaper before."

I grinned. "Then this will be good practice. Think of it as on-the-job training."

Mason put Brandon down into the little hospital bassinet and the baby started wailing.

He looked down at him with concern. "Why is he so upset? Do you think he's in pain?"

"He has a full diaper," I replied. "You'd cry, too."

"I should go get a nurse."

"Good idea. Get me some water too, please?"

He nodded and looked back at Brandon. "Listen… Daddy will be right back," he said in a serious voice. "Stay strong, Son."

I laughed and the baby cried even louder.

In panic mode now, Mason raced out of the room.

I leaned over the bassinet and caressed Brandon's cheek. "Don't worry. He'll get better at this."

For a second the baby stopped crying and I almost thought I saw a smile. But I knew he was too young and it was probably just a reflex.

"I bet you really do have a sense of humor," I said, smiling down at him. "You're going to need it with Daddy. Just don't be too hard on him, okay?"

Another loud gassy sound erupted inside of the diaper.

Grinning, I bumped my fist to his tiny one. "Now that's *my* boy."

The End

OTHER BOOKS BY CANDI HEART

Racing Hearts
Walking Dick
Love Handles
Big Escapes
Sweet Treats

About the Author

Candi Heart writes funny, sassy, and swoon-worthy romance that will leave you with a smile on your face and a sigh on your lips. She knows big, beautiful girls need love too, and enjoys writing about them finding their happily-ever-afters with sexy alphas from all walks of life.
She also loves hearing from readers! You can contact her at candiheartauthor@gmail.com, or find her on Facebook!
https://www.facebook.com/CandiHeartAuthor/

PINARD HOUSE
PUBLISHING

Made in the USA
Monee, IL
15 January 2022